חכמי ישראל בילדותם

STORIES FOR SHAULI

**Tales of Gedolim
when they were young**

חכמי ישראל בילדותם

STORIES FOR SHAULI

Tales of Gedolim when they were young

Rabbi Aaron Zakkai
Translated
by Judah Lifschitz

TARGUM/FELDHEIM

First published 1999
Copyright © 1999 by Judah Lifschitz

All rights reserved

No part of this publication may be translated, reproduced, stored in a retrieval system, or transmitted in any form or by any means, electronic, mechanical, photocopying, recording, or otherwise, without prior permission in writing from both the copyright holder and the publisher.

Published by:
Targum Press, Inc.
22700 W. Eleven Mile Rd.
Southfield, MI 48034

in conjuction with:
Mishnas Rishonim

Distributed by:
Feldheim Publishers
200 Airport Executive Park
Nanuet, NY 10954

Distributed in Israel by:
Targum Press Ltd.
POB 43170
Jerusalem 91430

Printed in Israel

ב"ה

THE YESHIVA
OF GREATER WASHINGTON

Rabbi Gedaliah Anemer		Rabbi Yitzchok Merkin	
Rosh HaYeshiva		Headmaster	
Rabbi Zev Katz	Sima Jacoby	Rabbi Zvi Teitelbaum	Arnold Brodsky
Principal, Judaic Studies	Principal, Secular Studies	Menahel Ruchani	Assistant Principal,
Girls Division	Dean of Girls	Dean of Boys	Secular Studies

OFFICERS

Melvin Rishe
President

Jeffrey Cohen
Avrom Landesman
Executive Vice Presidents

Emil Braun
Jack Delman
Samuel Franco
Aaron Lerner
Yitzchok Siegel
Abe Zwany
Vice Presidents

Shlomo Spetner
Secretary

Melvin Rottenberg
Treasurer

Michael Elman
Dr. Alan Goldman
Jerrold Hercenberg
Daniel Jacoby
Dr. Alan Kermaier
Trustees

Rabbi Kalman Winter
Chairman,
Vaad Hachinuch

Dr. Carl Posy
Chairman,
Board of Education

Bruce W. Herst
Executive Director

Tzivia Bramson
Administrative Assistant

כ"א חשון תשנ"ט

November 10, 1998

    Mr. Judah Lifschitz has again been מזכה את הרבים by translating the stories of the sefer חכמי ישראל בילדותם authored by Rav Aaron Zaakai of Jerusalem.

    Mr. Lifschitz has been able to capture in his preface the sentiments and feelings of the many members of our community towards Shauli נ"י and his family. Shauli has, indeed, elevated the spiritual level of our *Kehila* through the *tefilos, tzedakah* and *chesed* that have been offered on his behalf.

    May Shauli's dear parents, siblings and family, together with the entire community, merit to rejoice in celebration when the Almighty accepts our prayers and Shauli is blessed with a רפואה שלמה במהרה; a complete and speedy recovery.

בברכת התורה

Rabbi Gedaliah Anemer

UJA Federation Beneficiary Agency

BUSINESS OFFICES: P.O. Box 2125, Silver Spring, MD 20915-2125 (301) 949-7114 FAX (301) 949-7040
ARCOLA CAMPUS: 1216 Arcola Ave., Silver Spring, MD 20902 (301) 649-7077 FAX (301) 649-7053
GIRLS CAMPUS: (301) 879-8835 FAX (301) 879-8973

For Shauli, נ״י

שאול חיים בן אהובה אביבה
לרפואה שלמה

Aviva and David, עמו״ש
genuine friends who inspire us all

and

Eveline, Daniella, Daniel Kay, and Avigayil, שיחיו
the best sisters and brother Shauli could have.

Acknowledgments

I am thankful to the Almighty that He has enabled me to bring this translation to fruition and to publish the stories of *Chachmei Yisrael B'Yaldusam* in honor of Shauli and his beloved family. May Hashem enable me and my family to grow in the study of Torah and in the performance of mitzvos.

Rabbi Aaron Zakkai has graciously allowed me to translate these stories as well as other of his *sefarim* including *Heaven Sent: Stories of Faith and Effort* (Targum Press: Southfield, 1997). I am most thankful to Rav Zakkai for allowing me to make his works available to the English-speaking public. May Hashem bestow His blessings upon Rav Zakkai and his holy work.

Stories for Shauli is the product of the efforts of many individuals. First and foremost, my family has made the largest and most significant contribution. My parents, Morris, *z"l*, and Edna, *tb"l,* Lifschitz, have been a constant source of inspiration and support. So, too, my in-laws, Aaron and Paulette Feder, are distinguished role models. My extended family — my brother Karl and

Leah, my brother-in-law Elliot and Soshi, my sister-in-law Draisel and Gabi, and their families are important influences and examples, as well.

Most important of all, my wife Marilyn is always there by my side. She has enabled me to pursue many activities, often at her expense. She is responsible for the beautiful development of our wonderful three children — Pirchie, our dear son-in-law Yossie, and their little Moshe; Nachum; and Tamar. May these stories inspire them and their children to strive for spiritual greatness.

In the twenty-five years that I have been privileged to live in the Silver Spring community I have been blessed to be a student of our beloved *marah d'asra* and *rosh yeshivah*, Rabbi Gedaliah Anemer, *shlita*. When he first came to the community more than thirty years ago, Silver Spring was a religious desert. Years of Rabbi Anemer's hard work, perseverance, suffering, determination, and unwavering commitment to Torah and halachah transformed Silver Spring into a vibrant Torah community. Along the way, my life and those of many others were fundamentally changed. May Hashem grant Rabbi and Rebbetzin Anemer *arichas yamim v'shanim*, in good health and happiness.

I am also deeply thankful for the genuine friendship of my partners, Ron and Steve, my professional colleagues and staff, my dear friends, and most especially my *chavrusahs*. All of these people, each in their own way, guides me and supports me through the challenges of daily life. For this I am eternally grateful.

Lastly, a special note of appreciation to Moshe Dombey, my editor, Suri Brand, and the dedicated staff of Targum Press. My deepest thanks to everyone at Targum for making *Stories for Shauli* a reality.

Translator's Preface

Stories for Shauli is a collection of stories about *gedolim* and how they grew up. It is adapted from the Hebrew *Chachmei Yisrael B'Yaldusam*, written by the distinguished *rosh yeshivah* and author of numerous important *sefarim*, Rabbi Aaron Zakkai of Jerusalem. A few stories that could not be translated clearly into English have been omitted, and some changes have been made in the order of the stories.

These stories are for Shauli, an eight-year-old boy who lives just a few doors down the block from me. Shauli met with a terrible accident as a baby, *rachmana litzlan*, and has been very sick every since. I see him and his family often, yet in the years I have known him, Shauli has been unable to speak to me. He has never come over to play, nor has he ridden his bike past my house. He has never gone to school in the winter or to camp in the summer. Shauli has not been able to do the things the other children his age do. Instead, Shauli is tended to, night and day, by his devoted parents, nurses, and volunteers.

It was only a year ago that I first acquired a deeper (and, I believe, more accurate) understanding of the meaning of Shauli's life. He was in the hospital — again — in the intensive care unit at Children's Hospital, where he has spent so much time. I visited him and was greeted by his extraordinary mother whose anguished face told of an exhausted yet forceful determination to see Shauli through another life-threatening crisis. In her hands was a worn Tehillim. I thought to myself, *Does she really need the book? After seven years she must know Tehillim by heart.* We started to talk. Shauli's condition was critical. "*Hashem yeracheim,*" said his mother repeatedly. "May Hashem have mercy." Then she told me how upset she was that one of the nurses had suggested that the time had come to give up the fight.

"They don't understand. Shauli is not just a sick body. There is a *neshamah* in that child's sick body, and I am responsible for the care of that *neshamah.*" I shuddered then, when I first heard those words, and I shudder now as I repeat them. For it was upon hearing those words that I began to understand so much more about the meaning of Shauli's life.

I repeated to myself, *Shauli is not just a very sick child. He is a holy neshamah sent to this world for a holy purpose.... How many chapters of Tehillim have been recited because of Shauli? How many prayers have been offered by Jews all over the world in his merit? How many words of Torah has he caused to be studied? How many pages of Talmud have been analyzed on his account? How many minutes, hours, days of chesed have been performed because of this child?... How many people in the world have been responsible for so much merit among klal Yisrael? Who among us, except for our great gedolim, lives a life so completely dedicated to uplifting the spirituality of the Jewish people?*

It was then that I decided that these marvelous stories about our *gedolim* should be *Stories for Shauli*. Stories about young children who grew up to become great *gedolim*. Stories that inspire young and old to strive for spiritual greatness. Stories that remind each of us that we can, no matter what our circumstances may be, reach the heights of our spiritual potential, if only we try.

May the merit of this translation bring a speedy *refuah sheleimah* to Shauli and to all *cholei Yisrael*, and may the Almighty, the Father of Mercy, protect and care for the holy *neshamos* of Shauli and his family, who are extraordinary inspirations to all who are blessed to know them.

Contents

Rambam	17
Rabbi David ben Shmuel HaLevi	20
Rabbi Heshel of Cracow	22
The Vilna Gaon	25
The Or HaChaim HaKadosh	28
The Maharam of Lublin	30
The Chida	32
Rabbi Yonasan Eibeshitz	35
Rabbi Chaim of Volozhin	40
The Noda BiYehudah	43
The Maharam Schick	45
Rabbi Shlomo Zalman of Volozhin	48
Rabbi Yaakov Abuchatzeira	51
Rabbi Yisrael of Salant	54
Rabbi Meir Margolius	57
Rabbi Chaim Soloveitchik	60
Rabbi Shlomo Ganzfried	64
Rabbi Eliyahu Mani	67
Rabbi Shlomo HaKohen	69
Rabbi Yehudah Greenfeld	71
Rabbi Aryeh Levush	73
The Ben Ish Chai	76
Rabbi Shimon Agasi	78
Rabbi Rephael Chaim Moshe Ben Nayim	80
Rabbi Mordechai Leib Winkler	84
Rabbi Yom Tov Yedid HaLevi	87
Rabbi Eliyahu Yaluz	89

Rabbi Yosef Yedid HaLevi · · · · · · · · · · · · 92
The Chafetz Chaim · · · · · · · · · · · · · · · 94
The Or Yahel · · · · · · · · · · · · · · · · · · 97
Rabbi Yehudah Petiya · · · · · · · · · · · · · 100
Rabbi Asher Anshel Katz · · · · · · · · · · · · 102
Rabbi Kalpon Moshe HaKohen · · · · · · · · · 105
Rabbi Meshulam Igra · · · · · · · · · · · · · 108
Rabbi Yosef Tzvi Dushinsky · · · · · · · · · · 111
Rabbi Ben Tzion Meir Chai Uziel · · · · · · · · 116
The Chazon Ish · · · · · · · · · · · · · · · · 118
Rabbi Efraim HaKohen · · · · · · · · · · · · 121
Rabbi Rachamim Chai Chavitah HaKohen · · · · 124
Rabbi Akiva Sofer · · · · · · · · · · · · · · · 126
Rabbi Yaakov Gedalyahu Waldenburg · · · · · · 129
Rabbi Yisrael Zev Minzburg · · · · · · · · · · 132
Rabbi Avraham Shmuel Binyamin Sofer · · · · · 134
Rabbi Ovadiah Hadayah · · · · · · · · · · · · 136
Rabbi Ezra Ataya · · · · · · · · · · · · · · · 139
Rabbi Aryeh Levin · · · · · · · · · · · · · · 142
Rabbi Matzliach Mazuz · · · · · · · · · · · · 146
Rabbi Rephael Baruch Toledano · · · · · · · · 152
Rabbi Mordechai Amayis HaKohen · · · · · · · 154
Rabbi Shlomo Mutzfi · · · · · · · · · · · · · 156
Rabbi Chaim Sanune · · · · · · · · · · · · · 160
Rabbi Yaakov Mutzfi · · · · · · · · · · · · · 163
Rabbi Mordechai Sharabi · · · · · · · · · · · 165
The Baba Sali · · · · · · · · · · · · · · · · · 168
The Steipler Gaon · · · · · · · · · · · · · · 171
Rabbi Moshe Feinstein · · · · · · · · · · · · 176
Rabbi Yissachar Dov Goldstein · · · · · · · · · 178
Rabbi Yosef Adas · · · · · · · · · · · · · · · 180
Rabbi Michael Zerihan · · · · · · · · · · · · 182
Rabbi Shlomo Zalman Auerbach · · · · · · · · 185

RAMBAM

The Maimons were an illustrious family, who could trace their roots all the way back to King David. The Rambam's father was a student of Rabbi Yosef HaLevi, also known as the Ri Migash, a student of the Rif. Rabbi Maimon was a tremendous *talmid chacham*, who studied Torah day and night.

One night, in a dream, a stranger appeared to Rabbi Maimon and commanded, "Go to the next town and marry the butcher's daughter." When he awakened and remembered the strange dream, he thought to himself, *Dreams are often untrustworthy*, and put it out of his mind. That night, tired and weary from the day's studying, the strange man appeared once again and repeated his command: "Go to the next town and marry the butcher's daughter." Once again, Rabbi Maimon ignored the dream. But the stranger did not leave him alone. He continued to appear to Rabbi Maimon each night, until Rabbi Maimon decided to obey him.

He traveled to the next town and married the butcher's daughter. She died giving birth to their only son, whom they named Moshe. When young Moshe grew old enough to learn Torah, it was clear he was blessed with rare abilities. But he was lazy and did not like to study. Rabbi Maimon felt sad that his son was not following his example and started calling him "the butcher's son."

Moshe was very hurt and embarrassed by this. With a heavy heart, he left his father's home and went to the *beis midrash*. He cried his heart out before God and pleaded, "Please, Hashem, help me study Your Torah and do Your mitzvos." Moshe stayed in the *beis midrash* a long time, tears streaming down his cheeks, until he fell asleep on a bench.

The next morning, Moshe felt as if his heart and mind had been opened. He was interested in what he was studying, and his understanding was deep. A strong desire to learn Torah gripped him. While this feeling was still strong, he went to the *yeshivah gedolah* in Alexandria, which had been established by the Rif. At that time, the Ri Migash, Rabbi Maimon's rebbe, was the *rosh yeshivah* there.

When the *rosh yeshivah* tested Moshe, he was amazed at his new student's extraordinary abilities. Once he commented, "This young man will become great, and all of *klal Yisrael* will walk in his light."

Moshe did not study with the Ri Migash for long. The *rosh yeshivah* was old and frail. When he became ill, Moshe came to him in tears and kissed his hand. The great sage gathered his strength, placed his hands on Moshe's head, and blessed him.

When Moshe returned home, the happiness and pride Moshe's father felt at his son's turnaround could not be described. Moshe had left his father's house as "the butcher's son" and returned as a *ben Torah*, "son of the Torah." His father continued his Torah education, and Moshe worked hard. Eventually he became the Rambam we know of today.

RABBI DAVID BEN SHMUEL HALEVI

Rabbi David ben Shmuel HaLevi is best known as the author of *Turei Zahav* and was one of the leading authorities of halachah. When he was just seven years old he was an expert in *Bava Kama*, *Bava Metzia*, and *Bava Basra*. Because of his vast knowledge at such a young age, he became the youngest student in the yeshivah of Rabbi Yoel Sirkes of Cracow, author of *Bayis Chadash*. He had not even reached his bar mitzvah when he was accepted in the *yeshivah gedolah*.

Rabbi Yoel Sirkes liked this brilliant young man and invited David, along with a select group of students, to eat at his home every Shabbos. The rabbi had a daughter, Rivkah, who was beautiful and very intelligent. She was particularly well known for her extensive knowledge of *Chumash*. Once, during lunch, David remembered a line from Rambam's *Mishnah Torah* concerning the laws of writing a Torah scroll: "If a scribe had a word of ten or eleven letters on a line..." (*Hilchos Sefer Torah* 7:6). He asked, "In the Torah there are words which have nine letters — like the words *l'mishpechoseihem*, 'to their families' (Bereishis 8:19), and *laYishme'eilim*, 'to the Yishmaelites' (Bereishis 37:27). But which word has ten letters or more?"

Rabbi Yoel answered, "Let's call in Rivkah and ask her."

When Rivkah, who was then twelve years old, entered, David repeated his question. She blushed, uncomfortable at being the center of attention, and answered, "No word in the Torah has ten letters. But in *Nevi'im* we find a word with ten letters: *l'mishpechoseihem* (Yehoshua 18:21), spelled with a *vav*. But, of course, this has no connection to the law discussed by Rambam regarding the writing of a Torah scroll." She thought a bit more and added, "I think I have the answer. The law would also apply to writing a megillah. In Megillas Esther the word *v'ha'achashdarpenim*, 'the satraps' (Esther 9:3), has eleven letters."

Proud of his smart daughter, Rabbi Yoel stood up and said to her, "My daughter, you are as wise and as beautiful as the moon."

David Segal, the youngest student there, remarked, "It appears to me that the time has come to bless the new moon."

A small smile appeared on the rabbi's face. After Shabbos, Rivkah became engaged to the young student, who later became the *rav* of Austria, the author of *Turei Zahav*, and a great halachic authority.

RABBI HESHEL OF CRACOW

Rabbi Heshel of Cracow was known for his ingenious riddles, even as a young child. When he was four years old, his father once said to him, "Heshele, look at the difference between you and me. It took me a whole year before my shoes wore out. But in only half a year your shoes have worn out."

"Of course, Father," replied the child. "You are big and I am small. For each step you take with your large feet, I, with my small feet, have to take two steps."

Once, on *erev Shabbos*, Heshele's father said to him, "Here is a bottle. Go and fill it with wine for Shabbos."

Heshel took the bottle and asked, "Where is the money to pay for it?"

"Show me how smart you are. Bring me wine without any money," said his father.

The child left and in a short time returned with the bottle still empty. His father said to him, "What good is an empty bottle to me?"

Heshel answered, "What kind of feat is it to fill a cup from a bottle full of wine? Show me, Father, that you can fill the Kiddush cup from an empty bottle!"

One morning, before *cheder*, Heshel asked for salty fish and a piece of bread for breakfast. The head and tail of a salty fish were placed before him. His father said to him, "Here is an entire salty fish. Now go pray so that you can eat."

Heshel left, waited a moment, and then returned. "Father, I finished praying."

Angrily, his father said, "Heshele, what kind of davening is that?"

Heshel answered, "If a fish head and tail are the same as a whole fish, then '*Mah Tovu*' and '*Aleinu*' are the entire davening!"

Once, young Heshel found a roasted duck on the stove, waiting to be served for dinner. He could not restrain himself and ripped off a leg from the duck and ate it. When the duck with its missing leg was served, everyone knew Heshele must have eaten it. "Heshele," said the boy's father, "maybe you know where the other leg is?"

"Apparently," answered little Heshel boldly, "this duck was missing a leg when it was born."

The next day, Heshel and his father went for a walk. They reached the coast and saw a duck standing on one leg, its other leg hidden under its wings. The child said to his father, "Father, look at that! This duck also has only one leg."

His father lifted a branch and threw it at the duck. Immediately, the duck dropped its other leg and ran away. "Now you see that a duck has two legs and not just one."

Heshel responded, "That is true, Father. Had you done that to yesterday's duck, he also would have dropped his other leg."

When Heshel's father enrolled him in *cheder*, Heshel was not among the studious boys in the class. He did not like to go to *cheder*. The head of the school had to come and take him by the hand every morning.

"Heshele," his father would scold, "even the *yetzer hara* does what it is supposed to, causing people to sin. But you run away from your responsibilities and do not want to go to *cheder* and study Torah."

"Father," Heshel remarked, "what kind of comparison is that? The *yetzer hara* does not have a *yetzer hara*. I do have one, and it convinces me not to go to *cheder*."

When Heshel was six years old, he knew all of Tanach. Once, at the Purim meal, he was asked, "Why is Haman called 'Evil Haman'? Many other enemies of the Jews decreed the destruction of the Jews, and they are not called 'evil.' "

"Haman's wickedness," said Heshel with a smile, "was different. He chose to kill the Jews, not on Tishah B'Av, a day distinguished for punishment, but on Purim, a day set aside for happiness and feasts. He was so evil that he intended to ruin the joyous day of the Jews."

When Heshel was twelve, he was already looked at as a "miracle" because of his vast Torah knowledge. Many rabbis and wealthy men were considering him as a husband for their daughters. One famous rabbi said to him, "I've heard that you can discuss any page of the Talmud without preparation."

"That's right," answered Heshel with confidence.

The rabbi opened a Talmud to the very first page, on which, of course, there were no *gemaras*, and said, "What do you have to say about this?"

Heshel lifted the Talmud and rocked back and forth in silence while rubbing his thumb up and down the page as though studying it. Impatiently, the rabbi interrupted all this motion. "Well? I don't hear anything!"

Answered Heshel, "I don't see anything!"

THE VILNA GAON

Rabbi Eliyahu of Vilna was born on the first day of Pesach in the year 5480 (1720). By the time he was thirteen he had expert knowledge of *Chumash*, and he could recite all the prayers — including Tehillim — by heart.

On Sukkos 5484 (1723), young Eliyahu went to shul along with all the other *cheder* children, all taller and older than he was. At shul, one of the older scholars of Vilna decided to test the children's knowledge of *Chumash*. He stood up and said to the children, "It says in the Torah, 'An angel of God called out to [Avraham] out of heaven and said, "Avraham, Avraham" ' (Bereishis 22:11). Where else in the Torah is Avraham's name mentioned twice like in this verse?"

Before any of the children had a chance to even think about the question, Eliyahu jumped up and said, "In *parashas Toldos* it says, 'And these are the generations of Yitzchak, the son of Avraham; Avraham begot Yitzchak' " (Bereishis 25:19).

Everyone was stunned by the child's knowledge of *Chumash*. Another great scholar rose and asked another question. "Where, children, do we find a verse in the Torah that contains eight words, right after the other, which all end with the letter *mem*?"

The children concentrated and tried to recall the *pasuk*. But once again, little Eliyahu was the first with the answer. "The *pasuk* is in *Vayishlach*: '*Izim masayim u'seyashim esrim recheilim masayim v'eilim esrim* — Two hundred female goats and twenty male goats, two hundred ewes and twenty rams, thirty milk camels with their offspring' " (Bereishis 32:16).

Amazed at the child's memory, the scholar who had asked the question put the boy on his lap and held him close. "Tell me," said the scholar, "where in the Torah is there a verse that contains five words, one after the other, which have only two letters?"

Eliyahu thought hard for a few moments, then answered, "Actually, there are three such verses. In *parashas Bereishis* it states, '*Vayoled Noach es Shem es Cham v'es Yafes* — Noach begot Shem, Cham, and Yefes' (Bereishis 5:32). In *parashas Vayishlach* it says, '*Ki gam zeh lach ben* — You will have this son also' (Bereishis 35:17). And in *parashas Shelach* it says, '*Ki yad al keis Kah* — Because God has sworn by His throne' " (Shemos 17:16).

Once again the elderly scholar turned to the children in front of him and said, "You all know that there are three letters in the alef-beis that sound the same: *samech, sin,* and *sav*. Now, I would like each of you to give me examples of Hebrew words that contain each letter." The children started shouting out words, but couldn't come up with an answer for all three letters. Suddenly, above the din, young Eliyahu's voice could be heard: "In the *shir shel yom* for Wednesday there is a verse '*Binu bo'arim ba'am u'chesilim masai taskilu* — Understand, you boors among the people; and, you fools, when will you be wise?' (Tehillim 94:8). The last three words each contain one of the three letters."

The elderly scholar hugged and kissed the youngster. He danced with him in his arms, and soon the others in shul joined in. Old and young, hand in hand and arm in arm, danced in a circle, marveling at the young boy whose bright face shined with such intelligence.

THE OR HACHAIM HAKADOSH

Rabbi Chaim Ben Atar, known as the Or HaChaim after his commentary on *Chumash*, was born in the year 5456 (1695). He grew up in western Morocco, in the city of Sali near Rabat. Chaim was named after his grandfather, known throughout Morocco as a holy man for whom Hashem performed miracles and who was constantly learning Torah. The Jews of Sali called Chaim's grandfather "Father of the Orphans," because his house was a refuge for anyone in need, and he always gave generously to poor people. Often, while Chaim was lying in bed, he could hear his grandfather weeping and wailing over the exile and the troubles of the Jewish people. Tears ran down the face of the *tzaddik* when he lamented the destruction of the Beis HaMikdash, and his cries caused those who heard him to tremble. When Chaim heard his grandfather weeping, he swore in his heart that when he grew up he would leave Morocco for Jerusalem, where the Beis HaMikdash had once stood.

The Jews of Sali were captivated by young Chaim Ben Atar.

They predicted that he was destined for greatness. Even though Sali boasted many Torah scholars and saintly people, Rabbi Chaim stood out among them with his genius and saintliness. The respect Jews felt for him was evident when they added the additional word, *hakadosh*, "holy," to the title of his *sefer*, *Or HaChaim*.

Rabbi Chaim was removed from the physical world. Even as a young boy he would take it upon himself to fast for some reason or another. But these fasts never interfered with his studies, and he learned with extraordinary zeal. At a young age he wrote *Chafetz Hashem*, a collection of original insights on several tractates of the Talmud.

When he grew older, Rabbi Chaim became engaged to Patzonia, the daughter of Rabbi Moshe Ben Atar. Rabbi Moshe, a cousin of Rabbi Chaim's father, was a wealthy community leader from Meknès. Rabbi Moshe was also the king's personal advisor and accomplished many things for his fellow Jews.

After they married, Rabbi Chaim and Patzonia lived with the wealthy Rabbi Moshe. Rabbi Chaim soon became famous for his diligence in learning Torah and outstanding character. The Or HaChaim did not closet himself in his own private world, as he did when he was younger; he taught Torah and *mussar*, and in spite of his young age, many came to learn from him.

Rabbi Chaim Ben Atar's commentary on the Torah became very popular, and that popularity has endured. Today many still study *Or HaChaim* when learning *Chumash* or the weekly parashah.

THE MAHARAM OF LUBLIN

Rabbi Meir of Lublin, also known as the Maharam MiLublin, after the commentary he wrote on the Talmud, *Chiddushei Maharam*, was born in the year 5318 (1558). In his youth, signs of his genius were already evident. The elders of Lublin used to say that young Meir was a great scholar by the tender age of eight. He knew several tractates of Talmud by heart and constantly astounded his teachers with his original thoughts and insights.

Once he was sitting in front of his teacher learning *parashas Shelach*, that week's Torah portion. When he reached the part that dealt with the Jew who violated Shabbos in the desert by gathering wood, he stopped at the *pasuk* "And all the congregation brought him outside the camp and stoned him with stones, and he died" (Bemidbar 15:36). Meir's rebbe, who knew his young student's abilities, waited for the boy to continue.

After a few moments, the child's eyes lit up, and he continued reading. But the teacher interrupted him and asked, "Please tell me. Why did you suddenly stop in the middle?"

Young Meir answered, "When I read the words 'and stoned him with stones,' I was reminded of another *pasuk* in the Torah, which says that the punishment of someone who cursed is also stoning: 'And they brought the one who had cursed outside the camp and stoned him with a stone' (Vayikra 24:23). I wondered why it says that the wood gatherer was stoned with many stones, but the one who uttered a curse was stoned with only one."

"Did you discover the answer to your question?" asked the teacher.

"Oh yes!" answered Meir. "I remembered the comment of the *Ba'alei HaTosafos* in *Bava Basra* (119b). According to them, the wood gatherer did not gather wood in order to sin — his actions were for the sake of Heaven. At that time, the Jews thought that since it was decreed that they were not allowed to enter Eretz Yisrael, they no longer had to observe mitzvos. The wood gatherer desecrated Shabbos so the Jews would see what would happen to someone who sins and they would not act as he had done. Possibly, there were many opinions whether he was guilty or not. Some believed that he was a sinner, and when they threw a stone at him, they intended to kill him. There were others, though, who felt that the wood gatherer had acted with the right intentions. They did not personally think he should be stoned but did so because Hashem commanded it. Therefore, the Torah says 'and stoned him with *stones*' — to show that each one who threw a stone had a different opinion.

"But with the one who cursed, everyone had exactly the same view — that he be expelled from the Jewish people. Everyone recognized that he had desecrated God's name and that his punishment was stoning. Therefore, the Torah says, 'And they stoned him with *a stone*.' "

It is not surprising that this child prodigy became head of his own yeshivah when he was only twenty-four.

THE CHIDA

Rabbi Chaim Yosef David Azulay was born in the year 5484 (1724) in Jerusalem. His father was the *gaon* Rabbi Rephael Yitzchak Zerachiah Azulay.

As a child the Chida loved to learn Torah. While the other children played games, he would go off by himself to study. He realized that the true purpose of man in this world is to serve Hashem, and this was his greatest desire.

When the Chida was six years old, he began to study in Beis Yaakov, which had been established in 5451 (1691) by Rabbi Chizkeyah Di Silo, author of *Pri Chadash*. Rabbi Yonah Navon, his uncle, was a rebbe there, and young Chaim studied mostly with him.

When he was only eight years old, the tranquility Chaim always felt when studying was disturbed. An epidemic struck Jerusalem, and his mother fell deathly ill. For many days her condition was critical, and she lamented that she was unable to educate her young children because of her illness. She continually prayed for a speedy recovery. But she was comforted when she saw that her son Chaim was so dedicated to his studies and was receiving a proper Torah education in the traditional way.

Chaim, seeing that his Torah alleviated his mother's pain and agony, would talk about his studies. At the same time, he prayed for her recovery. But she did not get well, and on Shabbos, 8 Iyar 5492 (1732), she passed away.

Afterward, Chaim intensified his Torah study. His mother in Gan Eden would see that her son was studying Torah diligently and working on his *middos* as a legacy to his parents, and she would be comforted.

Before he reached the age of bar mitzvah the Chida began to write a commentary on the Talmud. His first commentary was on the *sefer HaGur* and on the laws of salting meat. Later in life, when he looked at his early writings, he wrote: "They are to be disregarded as the writings of a child...to be stored but not read."

By the time the Chida was bar mitzvah, he had studied the writings of the codifiers and halachic responsa. When his teacher, Rabbi Yonah Navon, left for a long journey, the Chida exchanged letters with him on halachic subjects and kept him informed about his studies. Rabbi Yonah was impressed by his student's clarity in his writings and encouraged him to keep up the correspondence.

In 5497 (1737), when Chaim was fourteen, his father married him off to the daughter of Rabbi Nissim Berachah, a great scholar who learned in Neve Shalom Yeshivah. His marriage to this beautiful, modest woman was a comfort to him after the loss of his mother at the young age of eight.

When Chaim was seventeen, he wrote his first *sefer*, *Sha'ar Yosef*, a deep and expansive commentary on the tractate of *Horayos*. This publication was among his most important works. It revealed his genius and the depth and the expanse of his knowledge of the Talmud and Mishnah. Rabbi Yonah Navon, Chaim's rebbe, described Chaim's extraordinary diligence, understanding, and analytical abilities in the introduction of the *sefer*:

"This Torah scholar, whom I know well, has strength and courage. Since his birth, he has been sanctified by Heaven. He is always immersed in Torah, in the laws of Abayei and Rava. He doesn't sleep at night, like a lion who is awake both by day and by night.... I love him with an everlasting love."

When the book was published fourteen years later, in 5517 (1747), three of the greatest Torah scholars of that generation disagreed with several issues. In response, the Chida wrote a separate pamphlet entitled *Achurei Tara*, which was later published together with the *sefer* itself.

RABBI YONASAN EIBESHITZ

From a young age, Rabbi Yonasan Eibeshitz of Prague was blessed with a mind as quick as lightning. He was able to answer any question he was asked correctly, sharply, and swiftly.

When he was three years old, his father, a rabbi, enrolled him in *cheder*. As was the custom, his father brought him to school on his first day wrapped in a tallis. The teacher took him in his arms and read to him the letters of the alef-beis, one letter after the other. Then the teacher read the letters backwards. The teacher was amazed when Yonasan immediately pointed to the letters with his fingers and read correctly the entire alef-beis backwards and forwards — with the proper pronunciation.

The next day, when Yonasan was brought to *cheder*, the teacher gave him a seat in the first row, where the four- and five-year-olds sat. These boys had already begun to read the letters with the vowels. The rebbe taught Yonasan all the vowels, and he learned them quickly. When the teacher reached the letter *peh*, he asked his students, "How do we read this letter when a *tzeirei* is under it?" All the children recited the answer together. "Don't any of you have a question about this?" asked the rebbe.

The children were silent, until Yonasan jumped up and said, "Why do we need a *tzeirei* under the letter *peh*? Even without it we would read it the same way."

The rebbe looked at the other children and said, "You should all be punished. This little boy, who started *cheder* just yesterday, is smarter than all of you."

"If they are supposed to be punished," said Yonasan with a smile, "then the rebbe should also be punished."

The teacher's face turned red with anger. "What?!"

"The rebbe should have asked this question earlier, when he read to us the letter *heh* with a *tzeirei* under it," said Yonasan, his face beaming.

By the time he was four years old, Yonasan already knew various laws and customs. He prayed each day and knew many of the prayers by heart. His father arranged for a *Chumash* teacher to teach his son, and after several months Yonasan knew all of *sefer Bereishis* by heart.

Yonasan was a mischievous child. His father would often get angry at his antics, but Yonasan, with his sharp wit, always knew how to explain away his behavior so his father would stop being angry.

Once, on a Friday afternoon, when his mother went to the market to buy a few items for Shabbos, Yonasan snuck into the kitchen where the Shabbos fish was cooking. He took a very large piece of fish, ate it all up, and didn't say a word to anyone. That night, when his mother went into the kitchen to serve the fish, she saw that a very large serving was missing. His father looked at Yonasan, his suspicion clear on his face, waiting for an explanation.

Yonasan was not scared. "Yes, I took the piece of fish. But didn't you teach me, Father, that it is a mitzvah to taste the food prepared for Shabbos on Friday in order to fulfill the prayer 'Those who taste it will merit life'?"

"But the mitzvah is only to taste," said his father angrily. "You did not have to take such a large piece."

Yonasan had a ready answer. "It also says, 'Those who love the Torah chose a large one' (Shabbos *mussaf*). So why are you angry with me?"

Once, during the Pesach seder, when it was time to eat the *afikoman*, Yonasan's father discovered it was missing. He figured that Yonasan was behind its disappearance. When he asked him about it, Yonasan readily admitted that he had taken the *afikoman* but said that he would not return it until his father promised to buy him a new suit right after the holiday. Left with no choice, his father agreed.

Once Yonasan returned the *afikoman*, his father handed out a piece to everyone at the table — all except Yonasan. His father told him, "I will not give you a piece until you release me from my promise to buy you a new suit."

Instead of agreeing, Yonasan proceeded to recite, "I am ready and willing to perform the mitzvah of eating the *afikoman*." He took a piece of matzah out of his pocket and ate it. "I figured, Father, that after I returned the *afikoman* to you, you would refuse to give me a piece until I agreed to release you from your promise. And since 'a wise person looks ahead,' I took my piece before I returned it to you so that you would have to fulfill your promise."

When Yonasan was seven years old, his father began to teach him Gemara. He started with the beginning of the Talmud, the tractate of *Berachos*. When they reached the *gemara* in the third chapter that deals with the issue of "a thought is like a statement" his father looked at him and said: "My son, our Sages decided that a thought is equal to a statement. I am thinking of a difficult question. Do you have the answer?"

"I am thinking of an answer," said the child. "Do you have anything that contradicts my answer?" Once again, Yonasan had outsmarted his father.

Aside from what Yonasan learned with his father at home, he was provided a rebbe as well to teach him Gemara. The teacher came to Yonasan's father to discuss with him which tractate he should teach. His father wanted the rebbe to teach *Beitzah*, but the teacher thought *Beitzah* would be too easy for Yonasan. Yonasan overheard the discussion. He went in and told the teacher, "You're right. The tractate of *Beitzah* could be too easy, but a *beitzah* (egg) can be either hard or soft, depending on whether one knows how to prepare it!"

Once, when Yonasan was seven years old, on his way to *cheder*, he met a notorious anti-Semite. The man, seeing a Jewish child, attacked him. At first Yonasan froze and started crying. But soon he regained his courage and thought of a plan to overcome his attacker. He pulled out the two coins he had been given to buy breakfast and gave them to his attacker. "Please take from me my meager gift. It is all I have. Today is a special day. It is customary that today if a non-Jew attacks a Jew, the Jew must give him all the money in his pocket."

The attacker scratched his head in puzzlement. Then a big smile crossed his lips. He took the money and went on his way. As he walked along, the non-Jew thought to himself, *It's too bad that I bumped into this poor young Jew today. If I'd attacked a rich Jew, I would have gotten my just reward.*

Just then, the anti-Semite saw the leader of the Jewish community approaching. The non-Jew rushed up to the man and began beating him. People heard the Jew screaming and came to help. The police soon arrived at the scene, and they arrested the attacker and put him in jail. The attacker declared his innocence and told the police that a young Jewish boy had told him that it was a Jewish custom on that day for non-Jews to attack Jews and receive a reward for doing so.

The police investigated and found Yonasan. They brought him to the police station and asked him, "What did this man do to you that you tricked him?"

Yonason told them what had happened and said, "I couldn't reason with someone stronger than me. So I decided to trick him. I was sure he would try to find a rich Jew to attack, and he would get caught and be punished."

Yonasan grew up to become a great Torah scholar and the *rav* of Prague.

RABBI CHAIM OF VOLOZHIN

Rabbi Chaim of Volozhin was the beloved student of the Vilna Gaon. Aside from his great knowledge of Torah, he had a sharp mind and possessed great determination and energy. He had a noble soul faithful to both God and his fellow man.

Rabbi Chaim's father, Yitzchak, was an affluent businessman. He allowed young Chaim, who had taught himself math, to assist him in checking difficult calculations.

Once, when Chaim was eleven years old, home from *cheder* to eat lunch, a beautiful chariot with four strong, handsome horses pulled up to his house just as he finished washing his hands and was reciting the blessing of *hamotzi*. The Count of Volozhin, who did business with Chaim's father, emerged from the chariot and entered Chaim's house. Chaim's father greeted the count warmly, and the count said to him, "Yitzchak, I did not come to discuss business. I want to ask your advice about a complicated calculation which has puzzled me."

"I am at your disposal," replied Reb Yitzchak.

Chaim, who had heard the count's request, stopped eating to listen intently to what the two men were saying.

"As you know, Yitzchak," the count was telling Chaim's father, "my father died two years ago. He left behind a lot of money and property to be divided among his three sons. As the oldest son, I have been busy with his estate. But there is one paragraph in my father's will which I have not been able to fulfill according to his wishes. My father had seventeen strong, handsome horses of which he was extremely proud — he used to show them off to his friends, to the other dukes and counts. He left the horses to his sons on the express condition that not a single horse be sold and that all seventeen be divided among his sons. I, the oldest, am to receive half of them. My next brother is to get a third of the horses, and my youngest brother is to receive one-ninth.

"If I am to get half of the horses, then I am supposed to received eight and half horses. If I could, I would sell one of the horses and simply divide the money among the three of us. But my father forbade us to sell one of the horses. And what about my brother's share of a third? That means he gets five of fifteen horses, but how am I to divide the remaining two horses into three? And my youngest brother, whom my father said should get a ninth, can receive one horse from the first nine horses, but how does he get his share of the remaining eight horses? We asked several attorneys for advice. They were all puzzled and could not resolve the problem of dividing the horses according to my father's will. So I have come to you, Yitzchak. They say Jews are smart. Perhaps with your intelligence you, or one of your friends, or your rabbi will be able to solve my dilemma."

No sooner had the count finished speaking when a young voice could be heard coming from the next room. "If one of the horses were harnessed to the count's chariot, I would be able to solve the problem easily."

Reb Yitzchak's face flushed red with embarrassment when he heard his child, whom everyone regarded as very bright, say such a ridiculous thing. The count, however, approached Chaim, patted him on his back, and said, "If you solve this problem for me, I promise that I will give you one of my horses as a gift."

A smile crossed Chaim's face, and he said to the count, "I have no need for horses, but I advise you as follows: Take one of the horses that is harnessed to your chariot and add it to the seventeen horses that have been left to you and your brothers. Together there will be eighteen horses. Then divide them up between you according to your father's will. The count will take half, nine horses; nine horses will remain. The brother who is supposed to get a third will take his six horses, leaving three. From these the youngest brother will take a ninth, two horses. There will remain one horse, which you will reharness to your chariot."

The count was amazed by the boy's genius, and Chaim's father was beaming. Before the count had a chance to express his amazement, Chaim had finished eating and had returned to *cheder* — on time.

THE NODA BIYEHUDAH

Rabbi Yechezkel Landau was well known even as a child for his wit. When he was twelve, he studied Torah with Rabbi Yitzchak Isaac Segal of Lodmir and lived with his father, Rabbi Yehudah HaLevi Landau of Afta.

At that time, the *gedolim* of Poland were debating a matter that concerned two brothers who were partners in a business. They had always conducted their business honestly together. But suddenly a time came when they fought with each other and separated. One brother promised himself that he would never see his brother again.

The other brother was so hurt by the oath that he became ill and died. The brother who still lived was very sad about the whole thing. He knew that it was his anger that had caused his brother's sudden death. He wanted to go to his brother's grave and beg for forgiveness. But then he remembered the oath — he had sworn never to see his brother again. So he went to the rabbis of his city to ask whether his oath was still in effect now that his brother had died. This question led to a tremendous discussion among the rabbis concerning the laws of oaths.

Yechezkel, who was twelve years old and already famous as the "prodigy of Afta," heard about this question from his brilliant rebbe. The boy said to his teacher, "I am amazed that our generation's *gedolim* are searching so hard to find an answer to this question. They have completely forgotten that there is an express verse in the Torah which provides a basis for relieving the brother from his oath."

His rebbe looked at his young student in amazement. "Tell me what you mean."

"It is very simple," said Yechezkel. "Moshe said to the Jewish people, 'As you have seen Egypt this day, you will not see them again anymore forever' (Shemos 14:13). Yet it says later on, 'Yisrael saw the Egyptians dead upon the seashore' (ibid., 30). Here is proof that when a person sees someone after his death it is not considered the same as seeing him during his lifetime. Therefore, the brother's oath does not apply after death."

Rabbi Yechezkal Landau became the head of the *beis din* in the city of Prague and the author of the *sefer Noda BiYehudah*.

THE MAHARAM SCHICK

Rabbi Moshe Schick, known as the Maharam Schick, was born on 21 Adar 5567 (1807), in the town of Razva Naytra, a small village from which many important people came. When he was a child, though he wasn't smart, he studied Torah diligently. In fact, later in life he told his father-in-law that when he was a child he had a difficult time understanding concepts. He could not understand Talmud even when someone else taught it to him. But he did not let that deter him from his studies. He would review his studies again and again, even if he did not fully understand them, even forgoing sleep. His great dedication paid off: God opened up the springs of knowledge for him, because, even more than understanding, the most important thing is a commitment to learning Torah.

Moshe was a frail child, and his doctors warned him that his long hours of study would make him sick. But he loved learning Torah and did not want to study less. His tireless commitment served him well, and in a short time he became known as one of the best students in the town. He became so well known that a wealthy man from his hometown convinced Moshe's father to send the bright young child to be his son's companion.

At the age of eleven, Moshe was sent to study in the yeshivah of his uncle, the *gaon* Rabbi Yitzchak Frankel, *zt"l*, head of the *beis din* in Ragendorf. In his uncle's house, he continued studying Torah with extraordinary diligence. Once, when his rebbe told him to go to sleep, he hid in a side room, covered himself with a coat to keep warm, and kept studying Torah. His rebbe was amazed when he discovered Moshe's hiding place in the middle of the night.

At the age of fourteen, young Moshe Schick was short and skinny. When he came to the Chasam Sofer's Pressburg Yeshivah, the first chance he had to discuss Torah with his new rebbe, the Chasam Sofer, was in front of the older students. They did not expect to hear the breadth of knowledge that came from the small boy.

The Chasam Sofer invited Moshe to eat at his home at the end of Yom Kippur. They discussed Torah over the meal, and the Chasam Sofer was so impressed he invited the boy to be his guest every Shabbos and *yom tov*. The close relationship Moshe formed with his rebbe, the Chasam Sofer, has few parallels in history.

For six years Moshe learned Torah from the Chasam Sofer. During this period he developed into an industrious, sharp, and extremely knowledgeable student. He was such a good student that the Chasam Sofer said of him, "I cannot offer him any new Torah insights because he knows it all," and frequently referred to him as a "trunk of books."

Moshe attained all this solely because of his diligence. In the Chasam Sofer's yeshivah there were many experienced, brilliant students who were extremely knowledgeable. When Moshe first came, he was well below their level. But with time he surpassed his friends. When he was asked how he was able to accomplish this he answered, "I reviewed my studies again and again until God had mercy on me and blessed me with a good memory and an understanding of what I studied."

When the Maharam Schick was the rabbi of Bergen, the Chasam Sofer came for a visit and entered the *beis midrash* where the Maharam Schick was giving a lecture on a *gemara* in *Sukkah*. The Maharam Schick did not realize that the Chasam Sofer had come in until he noticed his students gesturing to him that a distinguished visitor had come to see him. The Maharam Schick stood up for his rebbe and informed everyone that the lecture was over; he felt it was not polite to speak before his rebbe. But the Chasam Sofer told him to continue. The Maharam Shick completed the entire lecture, still standing on his feet, with lessons that he had heard from the Chasam Sofer. When he finished, the Chasam Sofer said, "You know, I had forgotten many of these insights."

There were times when the Maharam Schick repeated his rebbe's lectures word for word with the very tune that the Chasam Sofer had himself used, especially when he was studying *Chumash* with *Rashi*.

When he was close to his death, the Maharam Schick told his son that he still remembered everything the Chasam Sofer taught him and that everything he had heard from the Chasam Sofer, whether in halachah or in *aggadah*, was etched on his heart forever.

RABBI SHLOMO ZALMAN OF VOLOZHIN

Rabbi Shlomo Zalman of Volozhin was the brother of Rabbi Chaim of Volozhin and a student of the Vilna Gaon. As a child he was blessed with a phenomenal memory and a sharp mind. By the age of five he knew almost all of Tanach with *Rashi* by heart and prayed regularly in shul every morning and evening.

Once, a Jew from a small neighboring town came to the city of Volozhin. He went to shul for *shacharis* with his tallis, tefillin, and siddur. When the villager reached for his siddur, he could not find it. He suspected young Shlomo, only a child, had taken it. When one of the shul members, a *talmid chacham*, heard this, he scolded the villager. "This child is very careful in keeping the mitzvos. It is forbidden to think he would steal."

Five-year-old Shlomo had been listening to the conversation in silence, but now he interrupted. "Taking the siddur would not be transgressing '*Lo signov* — You shall not steal.' "

The elderly man who had been scolding the visitor stared at the boy, surprised. The other shul members, who had gathered around, were shocked. The child only smiled and explained, "Rashi explains that the *pasuk* '*Lo signov* — You shall not steal' (Shemos 20:13) in the Ten Commandments prohibits kidnapping. The verse that warns against stealing money is in *parashas Kedoshim* — '*Lo signovu*' " (Vayikra 19:11).

When Shlomo Zalman was seven years old he was already an expert in a number of Gemaras — *Bava Kama, Bava Metzia, Kesubos, Kedushin*. And he always stumped his teachers on Thursdays, when they learned the weekly parashah with *Rashi*. The week they learned *Chayei Sarah* and read the *pasuk* "Rivkah and her maids got up, and they rode on the camels and followed the man; and the servant took Rivkah and went on his way" (Bereishis 24:61), young Shlomo Zalman turned to his teacher and asked, "The Torah refers to Eliezer as 'man' in the beginning, when Rivkah and her maids followed him, but when he took Rivkah with him, he is called 'servant.' "

The teacher told his brilliant student, Shlomo Zalman, "*Nu*, my little Shlomo Zalman, you're smart. Answer your own question."

Young Shlomo Zalman closed his eyes, concentrating on finding an answer. "I think the words of the verse can be explained by a *mishnah* in *Kesubos* (48a), which I just learned. The *mishnah* says that a daughter must follow her father's customs and rulings until she gets married. Then she follows her husband. Once her father hands her over to the care of her husband's agent, then she must start to follow her husband's ruling, as if she is in her husband's care. The same is true if both the father and husband have agents. When the father's agents give her over to the husband's agents, she is considered to be under the care of the husband.

"The Torah's words are very precise," continued the child. "Earlier it states that Eliezer took with him 'all the goods of his master [Yitzchak]' (Bereishis 24:19). Rashi explains that Yitzchak prepared a list of everything he would give to Rivkah as a gift. This list included his servant, Eliezer — he would become the servant of Yitzchak's bride. When Rivkah and her maids first followed Eliezer, Rivkah was still under the care of her father. So Eliezer was not yet her servant. That is why the Torah says at that point that Rivkah and her maids went after the 'man.' Later, when Rivkah and Eliezer left without her maids, she was in Eliezer's care, her husband's agent. Then he was considered her servant, because that was Yitzchak's wish."

RABBI YAAKOV ABUCHATZEIRA

In the town of Risani, in the year 5567 (1806), a great soul came into the world — the soul of Rabbi Yaakov Abuchatzeira.

Rabbi Yaakov's father, Rabbi Masoud, was a great *tzaddik*. He studied Kabbalah and was known for his humility. Before his son was born, Rabbi Masoud had a dream. In the dream, he was told that he and his wife must purify themselves to be prepared to bring into the world a great person who would be the foundation of the world.

Rabbi Yaakov Abuchatzeira came from a distinguished, rabbinical family. The patriarch of the family, Rabbi Shmuel Abuchatzeira, lived in Damascus in the times of the Chida, Rabbi Chaim Vital. The Chida knew Rabbi Shmuel and wrote great things about him. He described how Rabbi Shmuel studied Torah all day in the synagogue and that he was known as a very holy man.

The family's original name was not *Abuchatzeira* but *Elbaz*. In Arabic the word *chatzeira* means "mat." The story is told that Rabbi Shmuel traveled by boat on his way to Eretz Yisrael. In the middle of the voyage, the boat capsized. As the boat sunk lower and lower, Rabbi Shmuel took a mat, threw it into the stormy sea, and sat on it. Normally a mat is not strong enough to hold a man and still float, but a miracle occurred, and the mat did not sink. He floated along until he was washed ashore onto the coast of Mogdir, in Morocco. News of the miracle spread through out the Jewish community of Morocco, and from then on he was known as *Abuchatzeira*.

It was clear from Yaakov's birth that he was a special child. While the other children played, he studied Torah or did a mitzvah. To Yaakov there was nothing more enjoyable.

Once a great Torah scholar came to Risani from Jerusalem. He stayed at the home of Yaakov's father, Rabbi Masoud, who was the chief rabbi of the city. The visitor noticed that Yaakov was studying *Bava Kama* and asked the boy several complex questions on the tractate. The child answered each question directly and to the point. Then the young boy asked the scholar from Jerusalem several questions. The visitor was amazed by the depth of the child's knowledge and understanding of the subject.

That a Torah scholar from Jerusalem could be so impressed was no small thing. In those days, men sent from Jerusalem to teach Torah outside Eretz Yisrael were extraordinary *talmidei chachamim*. The Jerusalem scholar went to Yaakov's father and said to him, "Your son knows more than I do!" The visitor stayed longer than he'd intended so he could spend more time with the boy and they could learn Torah together.

When Rabbi Yaakov became older, his father, Rabb Masoud, set up a special room for him to learn. Rabbi Masoud started discussing the halachic questions he was asked as chief rabbi with his son, Yaakov. In this way, Rabbi Yaakov was trained to be the next *poseik* and leader of the Jewish community.

Over the years, Rabbi Yaakov became well known as a holy man, held in high esteem by people worldwide. When anyone was involved in a dispute, even a non-Jew, he would come to Rabbi Yaakov to find a positive resolution. In every aspect of his life, Rabbi Yaakov sanctified God's name.

RABBI YISRAEL OF SALANT

In the Russian city of Zagar, in the year 5570 (1809), the *gaon* and *tzaddik* Rabbi Yisrael Lipkin, better known as Rabbi Yisrael of Salant, was born. Rabbi Yisrael's father was the great sage Rabbi Zev Wolf; his mother was the saintly Leah. Rabbi Zev, who was a teacher, taught Yisrael together with his other students. As his rebbe, Rabbi Zev imbued a tremendous love for Torah in young Yisrael.

The first signs of Yisrael's genius appeared at a very young age. He was blessed with a strong intellect, a quick mind, and an extraordinary memory. He loved to delve deeply into every topic he learned and understand it fully. He was full of ideas and would think up beautiful, original interpretations. Aside from his excellence in learning, Yisrael possessed a wonderful personality. He was pleasant and loved by all.

When he was five years old, Yisrael already knew by heart all five books of the Torah. Those who knew him were amazed at his quick grasp and extraordinary mind. At the age of ten he knew most of the Talmud with commentaries of both and *Acharonim*. Once he spoke in the large *beis midrash* in Zagar on a very difficult halachic topic. The scholars of the city came to listen to his talk. They asked him questions which he answered easily. At the end, they were amazed by the child's genius.

By the time Yisrael was twelve, the citizens of Zagar were all talking about his immense abilities. His father wanted to protect him from all the attention, so he sent Yisrael to study with his dear friend the *gaon* Rabbi Tzvi Hirsh Brodya, the chief rabbi of Salant. When the young boy came to Salant, he approached Rabbi Tzvi Hirsh and extended his hand to greet him. Yisrael then proceeded to tell Rabbi Tzvi Hirsh a complicated Torah thought that he had prepared by himself. Moved by the boy's words, the *rav* stood up and lovingly hugged the young Yisrael with great emotion.

In the first year that Yisrael was in Rabbi Tzvi Hirsh's home, a great Torah scholar visited and observed as the rebbe taught the boy Torah. The great scholar turned to Rabbi Tzvi Hirsh and asked, "Have you become a teacher of babies?"

"This boy is destined to light up the skies of the Jewish world," answered Rabbi Tzvi Hirsch. "Even today this boy is a 'small Talmud.' "

After his bar mitzvah Rabbi Yisrael wrote down some of his extraordinary Torah insights in a little pamphlet. On the advice of Rabbi Tzvi Hirsh, he sent it to the *gaon* Rabbi Akiva Eiger, who was quite impressed. After he read it, he commented, "This was surely written by an experienced *talmid chacham* who has acquired great knowledge. With his reasoning and understanding he can compete with the greatest rabbis of the last generation. I did not know that such a *gaon* exists in Salant."

Rabbi Akiva Eiger desperately wanted to know the identity of the great scholar who had sent him the booklet of Torah insights. Some time later, a resident of Salant came to Ponza, where Rabbi Akiva Eiger lived. He visited Rabbi Akiva Eiger, with greetings from Rabbi Tzvi Hirsh. Rabbi Akiva Eiger asked his guest, "Do you know a Torah scholar in Salant by the name of Rabbi Yisrael?"

"Yes," answered the guest. "This *gaon* is still very young. In fact, he just turned thirteen!"

"So young?" Rabbi Akiva Eiger was amazed, and explained about the booklet. He remarked that the Torah insights of this little *gaon* were as brilliant as any great scholar's. Thus young Yisrael made his mark and grew up to be the famous Rabbi Yisrael Salanter.

RABBI MEIR MARGOLIUS

The week Rabbi Meir Margolius started learning Mishnah, *parashas Bamidbar* was read. On Shabbos, after davening, Meir's father, who was the chief rabbi of the city, invited the leaders of Yazlovitz to a *kiddush*, celebrating his son's first lesson, a popular custom. They lifted the child to the tabletop, and he recited the *mishnah* he had learned by heart.

In the middle, Meir suddenly stopped. The *mishnah* reminded him of something. When his father asked him what he was thinking, Meir answered, "I had a question in *Rashi* in this week's parashah. It says, 'These are the generations of Moshe and Aharon' (Bemidbar 3:1). Rashi comments, 'It only mentions the sons of Aharon. They are called "the generations of Moshe," too, because he taught them Torah. From this we learn that the Torah considers a rebbe equal to a father.' According to the *mishnah* I studied, the power of a teacher is greater than the power of the father. It says there that the father only brings the child into this world, but the teacher brings the child into the World to Come. If so, how can Rashi write that he who teaches someone else's child is considered like his father? That would be lowering the teacher's status, not raising it."

Those listening to the little boy were amazed at Meir's insightful question. The boy's father looked lovingly at him and said, "Meir'el, you have asked a very good question. Now try to find the answer by yourself."

The child wrinkled his brow with concentration. Then his eyes lit up. He had found the answer. "I think Rashi is saying something different from what my teacher taught. Rashi's wording denotes an elevation of status. Rashi says *'ma'aleh alav hakasuv* — the Torah considers him.' *Ma'aleh* means 'to elevate.' This means that the rebbe is not considered the *equal* of the father. The Torah considers the rebbe to be on a higher level than the father."

When Rabbi Meir Margolius grew older, he became a devoted Chassid of the Ba'al Shem Tov. Once, the Ba'al Shem Tov said to him, "Meir, do you remember that Shabbos when you celebrated the first time you studied Talmud? What happened after you explained the *Rashi*?"

Rabbi Meir answered, "Yes, I remember it to this day. When I finished my explanation of *Rashi*, I wanted to go on reciting the *mishnah*. Suddenly, my mother stormed into the room, her eyes sad. She grabbed me and lifted me off of the table. Confused, my father asked her, 'Why are you taking him down? He hasn't finished.' My mother answered with anguish, 'There is someone here. He's wearing a fur coat, like a farmer does, and he's standing outside, staring at the boy through the window. I am afraid he will cast an *ayin hara* (evil eye) on him.' "

A smile crossed the Ba'al Shem Tov's lips, and he said to

Rabbi Meir, "I was the man who was staring at you. When I looked at your young face, I cast on you the light of Chassidus. That light caused you to recite a Chassidic explanation of the *Rashi*."

RABBI CHAIM SOLOVEITCHIK

The *gaon* Rabbi Chaim Soloveitchik of Brisk was the son of Rabbi Yosef Ber Soloveitchik and the son-in-law of the Netziv of Volozhin, Rabbi Naftali Tzvi Yehudah Berlin. The Netziv said about his son-in-law, "His abilities are greater than those of his father. He is a *gaon*, and his father is a *gaon*. He is saintly, and his father is saintly. But Rabbi Yosef Ber did not have a father like Rabbi Chaim has...."

When Chaim was a little boy, the great scholars of that time realized that a new star had been born in the Jewish world. He was very intelligent and a great wit. As a young boy, his hands were always dirty. Once his mother reprimanded him, "Oh, Chaim, aren't you embarrassed that your hands are so dirty? Did you ever see your mother with hands like that?"

Little Chaim answered, "Mother, I never saw you with dirty hands, but surely your mother saw you with dirty hands!"

When Chaim was five years old, his father would wake him early to go to shul and say Selichos. When Chaim showed no signs of getting out of bed, his father told him, "Chaim, the days of judgment are coming! Even the fish in the ocean tremble at this time."

"Yes, Father," answered Chaim. "But if the fish were sleeping in a warm bed like I am, they would not tremble."

When Chaim was six years old, Rabbi Yosef Ber sent him to a Chassid of the Slonomer Rebbe to learn Torah from him. Once, the Slonomer Rebbe came to Slotzk, Rabbi Yosef Ber's town. Chaim's teacher went to greet his Rebbe and took his little student with him. The Slonomer Rebbe looked at Chaim affectionately and gave him an apple, a real treat. Chaim grabbed the apple and began to eat it without first making a blessing over it.

"Chaim," said his teacher sharply, "no blessing?"

"You are responsible," said the Slonomer Rebbe to his Chassid. "Surely Chaim does not see you make a blessing before you eat something, and therefore he does not make a blessing either."

"The Rebbe is himself responsible," piped up little Chaim. "Surely my teacher did not see the Rebbe make a blessing before he ate, and therefore my teacher was not accustomed to making a blessing!"

Rabbi Yosef Ber once sent little Chaim to visit the head of the community of Slotzk with an invitation to the Soloveitchiks' home. The child entered the house and said to the the community leader, "The rabbi of Slotzk asks that you please come over to see him."

The man, who knew Chaim and loved to tease him, looked at him and said, "Chaim, why did you say that the 'rabbi of Slotzk' wants to see me instead of 'my father wants to see you'?"

"Because I did not want to say more than necessary. If I had said 'my father' then you would have asked me who my father was, and I would have had to tell you that he is the rabbi of Slotzk. So I just referred to him as the rabbi of Slotzk in the first place."

A friend, Zalman Sender Shapiro, who later became the rabbi of Meltz, used to study with Chaim and his father, Rabbi Yosef Ber. Once while they were studying, Rabbi Yosef Ber asked Chaim, "Tell me, son, which one of you is the better Torah student?"

Chaim answered, "Father, it is difficult to say. If I say that I am the better student, you will say that I am boasting. If I say that he is better, then you will say that I am a liar."

Zalman, who was also a clever boy, said, "I think Chaim is both a liar and boastful!"

When he was a child, Chaim found it hard to get up early to pray with a minyan in shul. Once, when Rabbi Yosef Ber came home from davening *shacharis*, he found Chaim getting dressed to go to shul. He said to Chaim, "Come see how great is the reward of those who wake up early to pray. This morning when I got up and went to daven I found a prize in the shul courtyard — a silver ruble."

Chaim thought about this for a moment and then responded, "To the contrary, we see that a person who wakes up early to pray loses. Obviously someone who woke up early to daven lost the silver ruble you found!"

As Rabbi Chaim grew up, his Torah knowledge grew. Of his particular method of study, his father, Rabbi Yosef Ber, used to say, "What is the difference between me and my son, Rabbi Chaim? If someone asks me a question on the Talmud or Rambam, both he and I get pleasure from the answer. When someone asks my son a difficult question, neither my son nor the questioner has any pleasure. I delve into the matter and research it, gaining new knowledge and the joy of learning. The person who asked the question is happy because he benefits from the Torah I've learned. But when a Torah scholar asks my son a question, he disputes the question immediately and shows why there is no basis for the question in the first place. So both the person who asked the question and my son gain no pleasure at all. The person who asked the question realizes that his question was foolish, and my son knows that there is really no question that needs to be answered!"

Rabbi Chaim eventually became the chief rabbi of Brisk and was known worldwide for his noble personality and holy spirit, his pleasant disposition and generous heart, his stunning intelligence and rare personality.

RABBI SHLOMO GANZFRIED

Rabbi Shlomo Ganzfried was the author of the *Kitzur Shulchan Aruch*. He was born in the city of Ungvar in 5564 (1803). His father was Rabbi Yosef Ber Zev Wolf, one of the most respected leaders in the Jewish community of Ungvar.

As a child, Shlomo was very gifted and obviously destined for greatness. In his Torah studies, he was well ahead of all his friends. Though Shlomo's father had to work very hard just to make ends meet, he spared no effort to make sure Shlomo had a proper Torah education.

Shlomo's father passed away when Shlomo was just eight years old. His mother now had to support the family herself, and they were very poor. Shlomo was sent to live with Rabbi Tzvi Hirsh Heller, the head of the Ungvar *beis din*. Rabbi Tzvi Hirsh, the author of the *sefer Tiv Gitten*, was known as "Reb Hershele the sharp one."

Rabbi Tzvi Hirsh raised Shlomo like a son. The rabbi inspired

Shlomo with his Torah, and Shlomo soon forgot all about his problems. His special intellectual abilities and amazing memory contributed to his great achievements in Torah. He accomplished so much that great Torah scholars quoted him in their Torah discussions. Rabbi Tzvi Hirsh had great respect for Shlomo and praised his young student's achievements.

When Shlomo was fifteen, he accompanied Rabbi Tzvi Hirsh to Binhad, where the teacher served as rabbi and head of the *beis din*. In Binhad Shlomo made a dear friend, Tzvi Hirsh Friedman, who later became the famous Rebbe of Liska and author of *Ach Pri Tevuah* and *Sefer Hayashar V'Hatov*. Shlomo and Tzvi studied together day and night. Their dedication to the study of Torah knew no bounds. Even their poverty, which caused them to go hungry from time to time, did not diminish their burning love for Torah.

With the guidance of their teacher Rabbi Tzvi Hirsh, Shlomo and Tzvi's Torah knowledge grew. They were able to fully research a Torah topic and determine the halachah. Over the years, their friendship deepened. In his *sefer Lechem V'Simlah*, Rabbi Shlomo quoted Torah insights from letters written to him by his childhood friend Rabbi Tzvi.

Eventually, Shlomo returned to his mother in his hometown, Ungvar. There he continued to study Torah. Rabbi Shlomo also assisted and studied with the *gaon* Rabbi Mordechai Mardish Weinreb, the head of the Ungvar *beis din* at the time.

Rabbi Shlomo married the daughter of Reb Yom Tov Lipa Madar, a leader of the community. Rabbi Shlomo's father-in-law, known for his piety and respect for *talmidei chachamim*, appreciated his son-in-law's greatness. Since he knew that Rabbi Shlomo did not have a job and was not interested in a rabbinical position, he gave his new son-in-law a large sum of money so he could open up a small business. This would give him time to learn Torah without worrying about how he would support his family.

Rabbi Shlomo settled in the city of Humna and opened a wine business. He ran his business honestly, even beyond the requirements of the halachah. But he was not successful and soon lost all the money Reb Yom Tov Lipa had given him. His father-in-law generously gave him more money to open another business, this time in Ungvar.

This time the business was successful, but Rabbi Shlomo's true interest was Torah. He studied Torah day and night as he always did. He was actually happy when there were only a few customers, because then he felt he wasn't being disrespectful to them by studying Torah rather than doing business. For him the word *kesef* did not mean "money" but "longing," from the word *kesufin*, as in the verse "For my soul longs for the word of the Lord; my heart and my flesh shall sing to the Living God."

Rabbi Shlomo's mother visited his store from time to time. Concerned that he might be neglecting his business, she would ask to see his sales records for the day. Rabbi Shlomo would open a drawer and spread out on the table, not his accounting books, but all the pages of Torah insights he had written that day. For him Torah was primary.

RABBI ELIYAHU MANI

The great sage Rabbi Eliyahu Mani was born in Baghdad in Tamuz 5584 (1823). His father, Rabbi Solomon, a charitable and kind man, gave generously of his wealth to the poor and to Torah institutions.

Rabbi Solomon hired the best teachers to teach Eliyahu, a diligent student with a sharp mind. As a young child, Eliyahu loved to do mitzvos. When he prayed, his eyes filled with tears. The *gaon* Rabbi Abdallah Somach, who later became Eliyahu's teacher, once saw Eliyahu crying as he prayed. After prayers Rabbi Abdallah came up to him and asked him why he had been crying. With youthful innocence Eliyahu answered, "I cried so that I will merit to study Torah diligently and so that I will understand what I learn."

When Eliyahu was a little older, his father enrolled him in Beis Zilkah, a *beis midrash* that had been established by Rabbi Abdallah Somach. In this *beis midrash* Eliyahu continued to grow in Torah and eventually wrote several original Torah insights.

His teacher Rabbi Abdallah was especially close to him and influenced him with his wealth of knowledge. Eliyahu's great desire to understand more and more knew no bounds. Later in life Rabbi Eliyahu described it himself:

"When I was fifteen years old, studying in the *beis midrash* of my teacher, I saw a man giving a book to my rebbe. I asked my teacher who this person was. He answered, 'This man has written a book and asked if I would give him a *haskamah*.' There are not enough words to describe the strong feelings that stirred in my heart when I heard my teacher's answer. For until that day I did not believe that there were people in our times who had the skill to write books about our holy Torah. That evening I left the *beis midrash* and ran all the way to the shul where Rabbi Yitzchak Gaon, a great Jewish leader of the Geonic period, is buried. I fell to the floor and, my tears falling on the grave of this holy man, swore, 'If God will be with me and give me the merit to write a book, then I will dedicate my first writing to Rabbi Yitzchak Gaon.' "

Rabbi Eliyahu kept his promise. The first book he authored, at the age of twenty-seven, was entitled *Siach Yitzchack*, named after Rabbi Yitzchak Gaon.

Rabbi Eliyahu married Serach the daughter of Yosef Kadduri, and they had a daughter named Rachel. This daughter married Rabbi Ezra Yechezkel Cohen, a student of Rabbi Abdallah Somach. Rabbi Eliyahu's life was a union of Torah, piety, and holy service to God and a stunning example of a generous, kind person whose special qualities shone through for all to see.

RABBI SHLOMO HAKOHEN

The *gaon* Rabbi Shlomo HaKohen, the author of *Binyan Shlomo*, was born in 5588 (1827) in Vilna. His father was Rabbi Yisrael Moshe HaKohen, a descendant of the family of Eili HaKohen (Shmuel HaNavi's mentor). Rabbi Yisrael was a great Torah scholar and a very pious man who studied Torah constantly.

Shlomo's father taught him Torah from when he was very young. As Shlomo later recalled in the introduction to his *sefer Binyan Shlomo*, he studied *Chumash*, Mishnah, and the entire *Talmud Bavli* with his father except for a few tractates, which he studied with his older brother, Rabbi Betzalel HaKohen. Rabbi Betzalel was a great Torah scholar in his own right — he wrote *Reishis Bikkurim* and *Mareh Cohen*, a commentary on the Talmud.

Before he was bar mitzvah Shlomo wrote a halachic discourse, which he later published in *Binyan Shlomo*. At about the time of his bar mitzvah he became ill, suffering terrible pains. The doctors warned him to rest and stop studying Torah, or he would surely die. Shlomo told them, "According to you, if I study Torah I will die. But if I do not study Torah I will die, because it is impossible to live without Torah. Better that I die from learning Torah than from failing to study."

Eventually Shlomo recovered from his illness. He studied Torah with renewed vigor with several *talmidei chachamim*, the most famous being Rabbi Isaac Shirvant, one of the leading rabbis of Vilna. For two years Shlomo studied *Choshen Mishpat*. Then he studied with the *gaon* Rabbi Yaakov Brit, a rebbe in a Vilna yeshivah. Shlomo studied in this yeshivah for several years, where he completed all four sections of the *Shulchan Aruch* with all its commentaries.

Great Torah sages had predicted that Rabbi Shlomo would become a great scholar and halachic authority. His brother Rabbi Betzalel HaKohen wrote, "My dear brother is like a tiger and an overflowing wellspring of Torah, Mishnah, and Talmud. He is like the young student who studied diligently in the *beis midrash* of Rav but did not consider himself great. He is a dedicated student of Torah. His name is Shlomo, and his knowledge is complete."

At the age of twenty-four, Rabbi Shlomo began to write down his insights on Torah, halachah, and the earlier and later codifiers. Over a four-year period he wrote an important work on several sections of the *Shulchan Aruch*, which was published later in his *sefarim Binyan Shlomo* 5649 (1888) and *Atzei Kerushim* 5660 (1901). He also wrote the *sefer Atzei Almogim* on *Choshen Mishpat*. Upon his death, he left behind some three thousand Torah articles and responsa.

RABBI YEHUDAH GREENFELD

Rabbi Yehudah was born in 5600 (1839) to Rabbi Shemayah Chassid. When Yehudah was ten years old, he went to live and study at the yeshivah of the Kol Aryeh, who became his main teacher, in the city of Mada.

Yehudah was very sharp. Though he was very young, he was a favorite student of his rebbe. Once he accompanied the Kol Aryeh on a visit the home of the *gaon* Rabbi Chaim of Tzanz. The Kol Aryeh presented his young student to Rabbi Chaim. Rabbi Chaim tested Yehudah on the tractate *Mikva'os* with the commentaries of the *Rash, Ram, Tur, Beis Yosef,* and the *Shulchan Aruch*. Rabbi Chaim was quite impressed. The Kol Aryeh remarked, "After this boy has learned a section in the *Tur* with the *Beis Yosef* and *Shulchan Aruch* only once, he can repeat it by heart." Rabbi Chaim added, "Please God, he will become a great scholar one day." This blessing was completely fulfilled.

Yehudah studied with his rebbe, the Kol Aryeh, during the

long winter nights from the beginning of the evening until the wee hours of the morning. One night, when they were learning diligently, the Kol Aryeh noticed that Yehudah was sleepy. He embraced him and said to him, "Tell me who really enjoys this world? The non-Jew who sleeps in the horse stable? No! We who learn *Tosafos* and new and beautiful insights. We are the ones who enjoy this world!"

When Rabbi Yehudah was seventeen, he was well known for his extensive knowledge and sharp mind. The daughter of a community leader, the scholar and *kohen* Rabbi Mordechai Kahana of Choset, was suggested to him as a *shidduch*. After he married, Rabbi Yehudah lived with his father-in-law for seventeen years. During these years he grew in Torah and piety and became well known as a great Torah scholar. Eventually he became the head of the *beis din* and yeshivah in the city of Simhali and wrote *Kol Yehudah*. He had a son, Shimon, who became a *gaon* in his own right, better known as the Maharshag.

RABBI ARYEH LEVUSH

When the *gaon* Rabbi Aryeh Levush, the rabbi of Kishnev, was only six years old he was already recognized for his sharp mind. He prayed with a minyan three times a day. In the evenings, after *ma'ariv*, he stayed in the *beis midrash* for the parashah *shiur* with Rashi's commentary.

During the week of *parashas Toldos*, the rabbi, as usual, gave his *shiur* with *Rashi*. When he reached the verse "The children struggled together within her" (Bereishis 25:22), he read Rashi's explanation of the word *vayisrotzetzu*, "and they struggled," out loud: "Our Rabbis taught that the word comes from the root 'to run.' When Rivkah passed by the entrance of the yeshivah of Shem and Ever, Yaakov would try to get out. When she passed by the entrance to a place of idol worship, Esav would try to get out."

One of the men listening to the lecture stood up and asked, "We can understand why Yaakov, when he tried to get out, could not — Esav was blocking him. But why couldn't Esav get out when he passed by a place of idol worship? No one was stopping him from getting out."

A small smile appeared on the teacher's face as he began to explain that this was the way the Midrash told the story, and we are not to question it. The man who had asked the question was not satisfied with this answer.

Suddenly young Aryeh jumped up and said, "When Rivkah passed by the entrance to a place of idol worship, Esav was surely trying hard to get out. But he was worried. If he went out at the entrance to a place of idol worship, Yaakov would then be able to get out at a place of Torah study, since no one would be there to keep him from getting out. So Esav decided to stay in his mother's womb just so he could stop Yaakov from leaving and going to a place of Torah study."

Everyone was delighted with the ingenious answer of six-year-old Aryeh.

Aryeh's parents found good teachers for their son. They developed his intellect and taught him Torah. By the time Aryeh became bar mitzvah he was an expert in Talmud and also had an understanding of Kabbalah.

On the day of his bar mitzvah, Aryeh delivered a long, complex speech. Afterward, one of the guests, a rabbi, asked him a question about a *gemara* in *Berachos* (14b). The *gemara* says that in Israel they did not recite the Torah portion of *tzitzis* in the evening Shema because the commandment to wear *tzitzis* does not apply at night. They would skip that part of the verse and say, "Speak to the children of Israel and say to them...'I am the Lord your God.'" The guest asked, "Our Rabbis taught (*Berachos* 12b) that 'every section of the Torah that Moshe divided we may divide. Any section that Moshe did not divide we may not divide [and it is thus forbidden to stop in the middle of a verse].' Therefore, how could the Jews living in the Land of Israel break up verses by saying only part of the first verse, 'Speak to the children of Israel and say to them,' and part of the last verse, 'I am the Lord your God'?"

Aryeh Levush, the bar mitzvah boy, had no difficulty finding an answer. "The two halves of these verses are really one complete verse elsewhere in the Torah (Vayikra 18:2). The Talmud means to say that in Israel they used this complete verse instead."

Thus was the cleverness of Rabbi Aryeh Levush at thirteen, who became the rabbi of Kishnev and a great *talmid chacham*.

THE BEN ISH CHAI

Rabbi Yosef Chaim, the Ben Ish Chai, was born to Rabbi Eliyahu Chaim on 21 Av 5593 (1832), in the city of Baghdad. When he was seven years old, he and his sister were playing in the basement next to a well, and he fell in. Crying, his sister went upstairs and told her mother that Yosef had fallen into the well. They rushed down to help him. When they removed him from the well, he wasn't breathing. They worked on him until he began to breathe once again. Thanks to Hashem's help, he had returned from death's door.

The elders of Baghdad used to say that Yosef Chaim wrote his first halachic responsa when he was just twelve years old. This was not a surprise; he was a diligent learner from a very young age. When he came home from the *beis midrash* he would hide in one of the rooms and review his studies quietly. Often his parents didn't even know that he had returned. He would go without eating until they finally found him later in the day.

Once, Yosef happened to see a letter sent to his father, who was the *rav* of Baghdad. The letter had been written by a Jerusalem *talmid chacham*. He had a question concerning the kashrus of certain *esrogim* and was asking Yosef's father to find an answer. Yosef had sneaked a look at the letter and wrote out a detailed and well-thought-out response based on the opinions of the great codifiers. Without telling his father, he mailed the letter to the scholars of Jerusalem. Several days later, when the scholars in Jerusalem received a response from Rabbi Eliyahu himself, they wrote him the following letter: "Your son, Yosef, has already answered our question. A smart son will make his parents who gave birth to him happy."

Another time, Yosef Chaim became famous when there were no *esrogim* to be found in the entire city of Baghdad for the holiday of Sukkos except for a single *esrog* that had grown in an orchard owned by some underage orphan. In the study halls of Baghdad, scholars delved into the question of whether the orphan's trustee could legally sell the *esrog* for the underage orphan, since the Torah required that the *esrog* one uses on Sukkos be his own. Sukkos was approaching, and the scholars could not reach a decision. They gathered in the home of Yosef Chaim, who was by then a well-known young scholar, to ask his opinion.

Yosef Chaim hurried to the attic and spent the night searching through the Talmud and Mishnah. In the morning, several scholars came to hear his decision. Yosef Chaim piled in front of them all the *sefarim* he had used for his research, two hundred in number, and said to them, "See for yourselves what is written and decide. I, myself, cannot permit it. In my opinion, there is no possibility that one can make a blessing on such an *esrog* on the first day of Sukkos, and I will not do so." And so it was. Not a single Jew in Baghdad made the blessing over an *esrog* that year, in accordance with the decision of Rabbi Yosef Chaim.

RABBI SHIMON AGASI

Rabbi Shimon Agasi was born in the city of Baghdad in the year 5612 (1851). His father was Rabbi Aharon, the son of Rabbi Abba Agasi, whose father's name was also Abba.

The family originally came from Persia. The first Rabbi Abba traveled often from Persia to Baghdad for business. Eventually he established his home there. According to the family tradition, Rabbi Abba passed away before his son was born, and his son was named after him.

The family name comes from the Persian word *aga*, which means "commissioner." They got that name because the family was close to the royal family and the government.

Rabbi Aharon Agasi, Shimon's father, had a dye business. He specialized in a certain dye that came from India. His sons also worked in the business and traveled to other cities and towns to sell the dye.

Baghdad was undergoing an economic revolution at the

time. The opening of the Suez Canal in 5629 (1868) broadened the economic ties between Baghdad and Europe. The discovery of oil in Iraq, steamships which began to voyage on the Euphrates River connected the large economic centers of different cities, European businessmen who came regularly to Baghdad — all these factors caused the majority of Jewish children to leave their studies in the *beis midrash* at the age of thirteen and go into their parents' or relatives' businesses.

But Shimon Agasi was not interested in all that. Like every young Jewish child he studied with a teacher. By age eleven he had studied the entire Tanach many times. He knew several chapters of Talmud perfectly, spoke Hebrew fluently, and was able to write Hebrew in the Babylonian Jewish tradition. When he became thirteen, unlike other boys his age, he had no interest in the world of business. His heart's desire was to learn and understand the wisdom of the Torah and to dedicate himself to studying the Torah's secrets. He also kept his distance from the boys who continued their studies in the school established in 5625 (1864) by the organization Kol Yisrael Chaveirim. This school caused many Jewish children to leave the path of their fathers.

Shimon studied day and night in the *beis midrash* Beis Zilkah, established by the *gaon* Rabbi Abdallah Somach. Since business was secondary for him, he devoted only a small part of his day to working for his father. His brothers were not pleased with this. They began to complain that young Shimon was not carrying his weight. But his parents were thrilled with the idea of Shimon becoming a Torah scholar. With the passage of time Shimon's parents decided to establish the name of their family endeavor after the name of their great son Rabbi Shimon.

RABBI REPHAEL CHAIM MOSHE BEN NAYIM

At the end of the year 5605 (1844), a boat from Africa docked at the small port of Haifa. On board were Jewish families who were emigrating to the Land of Israel from Morocco. Among these families was Rabbi Yeshayah Ben Nayim, with his wife and six-month-old son, Moshe. They had traveled from Titan, a city in eastern Morocco. This baby was destined to become the great Torah scholar and sage Rabbi Rephael Chaim Moshe Ben Nayim, known by all the Mediterranean Sephardic Jewish communities as *HaRav HaRachaman*, "the Merciful Rabbi."

Life in Israel was difficult for the Ben Nayim family. They had little money and were hoping that in Haifa they would be able to earn a livelihood. But there were few *sefarim* and only one rebbe to teach Torah to all the children of Haifa. So when Moshe was old enough to go to school, he learned *Chumash* with this rebbe. Moshe's father, Rabbi Yeshayah, taught Moshe some *aggadah*, halachah, and *Zohar* at night and during his free moments. Moshe learned how to write from one of the nearby storekeepers, and when he was eleven, he became a shopowner's assistant. His parents were not happy with this situation. But they could not afford to live in a place where Moshe could study Torah and become a great *talmid chacham*.

At that time, a great rabbi named Rabbi David Ben Shimon lived in Jerusalem. He was known as Devash, which is the Hebrew word for "honey." This rabbi had established a *beis din*, yeshivah, and elementary school for the members of his community. Among the residents of Jerusalem he was known as "the father of orphans and the judge of widows" because of his many extraordinary activities on behalf of destitute people. He also founded a neighborhood known as Machaneh Yisrael, outside the Old City walls of Jerusalem. In the center of Machaneh Yisrael was a synagogue known as Tzuf Devash.

One day Rabbi David Ben Shimon came to Haifa and saw the young boy, Moshe Ben Nayim, sitting in a store. This great rabbi could not contain himself. He asked Moshe's father, Rabbi Yeshayah, why he had taken his son away from his studies. With a heavy heart, Rabbi Yeshayah explained that there were no scholars in Haifa to teach older boys like Moshe Torah, and he could not afford to send Moshe out of town.

Rabbi David took out a small *Ein Yaakov*, which he kept in his pocket, and asked Moshe to read from it and explain what he was reading. The boy read it fluently and explained it as well as he could. The Devash realized that Moshe had the potential to become a great scholar. He asked Rabbi Yeshayah for permission to take Moshe with him to Jerusalem. There he would take care of all of his needs. Moshe would live with him and study with his sons until he became the Torah scholar he was meant to be.

Though Moshe's mother wanted him to study Torah, she did not want to allow the rabbi to take him to Jerusalem. It was very difficult to travel from Haifa to Jerusalem. One had to take a boat from Haifa to Jaffa and then ride by donkey to Jerusalem. She was afraid it would be too much for the boy.

Rabbi David would not give up. Finally Moshe's parents promised that when he reached the age of bar mitzvah, they would send him to Tiberias, which was much closer and had yeshivos. Rabbi David was satisfied, and he gave his blessing.

A few short months after Rabbi David Ben Shimon's visit, Moshe celebrated his bar mitzvah. Immediately after the celebrations, his father took him to Tiberias. There he found Torah scholars to teach Moshe and arranged lodgings for the boy. His parents sent Moshe money for his expenses and were pleased that their only son was studying Torah. Moshe's main teacher was Rabbi Chaim Shmuel Kunvarti, the leading Torah scholar in Tiberias. Soon the boy's reputation as a scholar grew among the *talmidei chachamim* of Tiberias, a city where some of the greatest sages of the time lived.

From time to time Moshe would travel to Haifa to visit his parents. During one visit, in the summer of 5620 (1859), he became very sick. The doctors practically gave up all hope. Two names, *Rephael* and *Chaim*, which mean "Hashem heals" and "life," were added to his name. After several days his condition improved — he gained strength and regained his health. Sadly, Moshe's saintly mother then became ill, and after a few days she passed away.

After the year of mourning, when Moshe was sixteen years old, he married Rachel, the modest and fine daughter of Rabbi Shmuel Yisrael. Rachel was an orphan, so Rabbi Yeshayah took care of all the wedding arrangements. After the wedding, which took place in Haifa, the couple returned to Tiberias. Rabbi Yeshayah continued to support them so his son could learn Torah in peace and serve the Almighty.

RABBI MORDECHAI LEIB WINKLER

Rabbi Mordechai Leib Winkler was the author of *Levushei Mordechai*. He was born in 5604 (1843) in the town of Lifnitvitz, Slovakia.

This great sage and scholar was born into a simple family. Neither his father, Naftali Hirtz, nor his mother, Leah, came from a rabbinical or well-known family. They were honest, God-fearing people who worked hard to make ends meet. Though Naftali Hirtz was busy all week trying to make a living, everywhere he went he recited *tehillim*. Leah was dedicated to raising good Jewish children who would grow up to serve God. There was no rebbe to teach the children Torah, so she herself taught them alef-beis and how to read Hebrew. She wanted them to learn more, but she only knew some *Chumash*, which she could translate into Yiddish with some explanations and *midrashim*.

When Mordechai was six years old, he did not play much

with the other children. Every morning his mother took him to the *cheder* in Nytra, and every evening she picked him up. When he was twelve years old, Mordechai went to learn in the yeshivah of the *gaon* Rabbi Wolf Tirzhes, the head of the *beis din* in Tephalsthan.

At the yeshivah, Mordechai ate very little during the week and was physically very weak. But spiritually he was strong. He learned by heart the tractates of *Bava Kama* and *Bava Metzia* and wrote down many original Torah insights.

Eventually he went to study with Rabbi Mordechai Yehudah Glick, the head of the Yahani *beis din*, but he did not stay there for very long. He walked from there to the large city of Grossvarden to learn in the yeshivah of the *gaon* Rabbi Yisrael Yitzchak Aharon Landsburg. He received his rabbinical ordination from Rabbi Yisrael Yitzchak, the great *tzaddik* Rabbi Meir Perlas, and the *gaon* Rabbi Avraham Yissachar Ber Leichtag. Mordechai wrote about these three sages:

"I merited to serve great scholars, all students of the Chasam Sofer. With Hashem's help, their method of clear thinking and their interpretations of the Talmud, *Rashi*, *Tosafos*, and the other commentaries made a lasting impression on me to teach students in the same manner."

When he reached marriageable age, Rabbi Mordechai married Rivkah, the daughter of Rabbi Menachem Mendel Krauss. His father-in-law appreciated his special qualities and worked hard to support him and take care of his needs. For two years after he married, Rabbi Mordechai and his wife lived with the Krauss family, and he learned Torah.

Eventually Rabbi Mordechai opened a small store in Grossvarden, but the business made no profit. If Rabbi Mordechai saw that a customer was poor and could not afford to pay, he would give him everything for free. He called it a loan so they would not feel embarrassed, though he knew they could not pay him back. After nine months he had to close down the store.

Now Rabbi Mordechai had no livelihood. His beloved teacher Rabbi Yitzchak Aharon Landsburg came to his rescue and offered him a position as rabbi of a community in the north called Maza Telgad. In the year 5634 (1875), his rebbe invited him to visit the town. Rabbi Yitzchak Aharon went up to the *bimah* in the *beis midrash* and spoke to the community.

"You are now a beautiful community that can afford to maintain, with a minimum of difficulty, my student as your rabbi. He is worthy of this position. Make him your *rav*."

The community of Maza Telgad did not regret listening to Rabbi Yitzchak Aharon. Rabbi Mordechai opened a yeshivah there, where he studied and taught the word of God to students who came from near and far.

RABBI YOM TOV YEDID HALEVI

The *gaon* and Kabbalist Rabbi Yom Tov Yedid HaLevi was one of the great Torah scholars of Aram Soba, Syria. The scope of his knowledge spanned both traditional Torah texts as well as its mystical subjects. He taught many students and served his fellow Jews for twenty-seven years. All that time he prayed out of the siddur of the Rashash. Eventually he published this siddur in nine volumes with his own commentary.

Rabbi Yom Tov was always the first to reach the synagogue or *beis midrash*. His son, Rabbi Eliezer Yedid, who was also a Torah scholar, wrote in his *sefer Shivchei Maharit*: "When I was a young boy, I would go with my father to pray in the synagogue Mechuvanim in the Rechovot neighborhood of Jerusalem. After prayers, when everyone else would go home, he would remain in shul. I used to say to him, 'Everyone else in the congregation has gone home. Why don't we go, too?' He would answer, 'The house is not running away. But sitting in the synagogue is a mitzvah. And every moment we sit here we get a bigger mitzvah.'"

Rabbi Yom Tov's diligence in Torah study knew no bounds. His son Rabbi Eliezer wrote, "His exceptional diligence in Torah study, day and night, was evident even when he was a young boy. It was as if the rest of the world were nothing but foolishness to him."

His faith in the Almighty was exceptionally strong. As his son Rabbi Eliezer described, "Once the prices for food in the market went up, and Torah scholars could not afford to buy food. Somehow they managed to obtain some flour to distribute to Torah scholars and poor people. They notified the Torah scholars that they should come to a certain place to pick up the flour. But my great father did not move an inch from his place in the *beis midrash*. People asked him, 'Why don't you send someone to pick up your share of flour?' He answered, 'Every person will get what has been set aside for him. And if it is God's will to give me some flour, He will send it to me.' And so it was. A wealthy man came into the *beis midrash* and gave my father two gold coins. The man said he should come back to him when he had spent this money, and he would give him some more. This continued for several years."

Rabbi Eliezer continued, "When he would hear people speaking about how much money someone had, for example, 'That person has a large house,' or 'So-and-So is wealthy,' he would say to them, 'I am wealthier than all of them, because this whole neighborhood belongs to me.... But you should know that I have heavy taxes and I owe debts to the government, besides my other expenses. So what good is all my wealth? The most important thing is that a person is satisfied with what he has....'"

On the Wednesday afternoon before he passed away, on 30 Sivan 5683 (1923), there was a thunderstorm, and all the low spots in the city were flooded. Everyone in the city said they had never seen so much rain in the middle of the summer, which is the dry season in Israel. When Rabbi Yom Tov Yedid passed away, the weather again became pleasant, as it had been before he died.

RABBI ELIYAHU YALUZ

Rabbi Eliyahu Yaluz was born in Elul 5620 (1860) in Mazgira, located in central Morocco. His father was Rabbi Avraham Yaluz, and his mother was Chanah, the daughter of a wealthy and God-fearing businessman. Chanah once told her grandson Rabbi Yosef Chaim that before she became pregnant, Eliyahu HaNavi came to her in a dream and said, "Chanah, you will give birth to a son who will light up the eyes of the Jewish people in Torah. The sign that what I say will come true is that he will be born already circumcised. Name him Eliyahu after me." And so it was.

Rabbi Avraham was a goldsmith, as were many Moroccan Jews. Since he worked all day, he taught Eliyahu Torah at night. For Eliyahu's daytime studies, Rabbi Avraham hired a teacher. By the time the boy was seven years old, he understood *Ein Yaakov* and *Chok L'Yisrael*. By the time he was twelve, everyone knew about young Eliyahu's remarkable intellect and sharpness.

Once, during a Shabbos meal, Eliyahu's father asked him to

recite an original Torah idea on that week's parashah, *Yisro*. Young Eliyahu said, "The first letters of the verse 'Remember the Sabbath to keep it holy' is numerically equal to the words *eliyahu* and *yaluz*. This means that Eliyahu Yaluz must 'remember the Sabbath to keep it holy' by saying *divrei Torah*."

Rabbi Avraham was delighted with the *vort*. He hugged his son and planted a kiss on his forehead. Soon after, Rabbi Avraham visited the rabbi of the city, the *gaon* Rabbi Yaakov Abuchatzeira, to speak to him about his son. The rabbi blessed Eliyahu that God should protect him from any harm and that he should grow up to be a Torah scholar and teacher. The blessing of the great rabbi did indeed come true.

In the beginning of the year 5633 (1872), when Eliyahu was twelve years old, his father told Rabbi Yaakov Abuchatzeira that he wanted to move to Israel. The rabbi encouraged him, quoting Hashem's words to Avraham Avinu when he commanded him to go to the promised land: "Avraham, leave your land and birthplace and go to the holy land."

Eliyahu's father sold all his belongings, closed his business, and set out for Israel with his family. When he reached the city of Pass, the sultan Muhammad died. Travel became very dangerous, because criminals took advantage of the chaos a monarch's death brought. With no choice, the Yaluz family waited in Pass for a full year until a new sultan, Mulay Alchasan, came to power and the situation was more stable.

Eliyahu celebrated his bar mitzvah in Pass. He gave a long speech on the parashah, amazing his listeners with his brilliance.

With the political situation more settled, Rabbi Avraham and his family continued their journey. They passed through Tangiers and Alexandria, Egypt. Eventually they reached the port of Haifa. From there they went to their final destination, Tiberias, which they reached in Teves 5634 (1874).

When Eliyahu came to Tiberias, he searched for friends with whom he could study and sought the scholars of the city to be his teachers. Very quickly, he became known as a young, very accomplished child prodigy.

To Eliyahu's great sorrow, his father, Rabbi Avraham, died soon after they settled in Tiberias. He was in the prime of his life when he passed away in Tamuz 5635 (1875), only a year after the family had arrived in Israel.

After the year of mourning, when Eliyahu was just sixteen years old, he gave a brilliant lecture before the great Torah scholars and rabbis of Tiberias. Later, he published this speech in his *sefer Pesach Eliyahu*. From then on, the Jews of Tiberias recognized that Eliyahu was destined for greatness. A year later, at the age of seventeen, Eliyahu married the daughter of Tiberias scholar Rabbi David Asudri. On his wedding day Eliyahu gave a brilliant speech, which was published in the introduction to *Pesach Eliyahu*.

He also authored the *sefer Yeish MeiAyin* and served as the head of the *beis din* of Tiberias for over forty years. He wrote many beautiful articles until he passed away in 5689 (1929).

RABBI YOSEF YEDID HALEVI

The *gaon* Rabbi Yosef Yedid HaLevi was the head of the *beis din* for the Syrian and Bucharin communities in Jerusalem. He was born in Aram Soba, Syria, in 5627 (1876).

Yosef's father, Rabbi Mordechai, was a poor teacher of young children. Yosef helped his father teach the children, but after a few years, Yosef realized that teaching was taking away from his own studies. He had a burning desire to study Torah, particularly Mishnah, Gemara, and halachah. But he could not afford to pay a teacher. Every evening, after Yosef finished helping his father with the children, he would go to the synagogue, open up the *aron kodesh*, and cry to the Almighty for help so he would be able to study Torah.

Once, the *gaon* and Kabbalist Rabbi Shaul Katzin saw Yosef crying and praying in the synagogue before the open ark. Rabbi Katzin approached Yosef and asked him why he was so upset. Yosef explained how he felt he was spending so much time helping his father that he was not able to advance in his own studies. His real desire was to study Talmud and Mishnah. But his father was not able to help him because he did not have enough money.

Rabbi Shaul Katzin calmed Yosef down. He said he would try to make it possible for him to study as he wished.

Rabbi Katzin went to several wealthy and generous people and asked them to contribute money so that Yosef could study with a rabbi. That day Yosef began to study Torah and never stopped. He advanced a great deal in his studies and eventually became a great Torah scholar.

Rabbi Yosef studied in Aram Soba with Rabbi Avraham Adas. His study partner was Rabbi Ezra Sharim. The two were very serious about their studies. They both became members of the *beis din* and teachers.

In 5650 (1890), Rabbi Yosef immigrated to Israel and settled in the holy city of Safed. There he studied Torah with great intensity. He wrote the first volume of *Toras Chacham* and met his cousin, the saintly Kabbalah scholar Rabbi Yom Tov Yedid HaLevi, who suggested that he move to Jerusalem. The Bucharin community offered Rabbi Yosef a position as a *dayan* and teacher, and after a while he was appointed *dayan* for the Aram Soba community as well.

Rabbi Yosef Yedid was blessed with many students who followed his path. Among them was Rabbi Raphael Shlomo Landau and Rabbi Ezra Ataya, both of whom later became the *roshei yeshivah* of Porat Yosef in Jerusalem.

THE CHAFETZ CHAIM

Rabbi Yisrael Meir HaKohen was the author of the monumental works *Chafetz Chaim* and *Mishnah Berurah*. He was born in the city of Zital near Slonim, Poland, on 11 Shevat 5599 (1839).

When the Chafetz Chaim was ten years old, he traveled to Vilna to study. When he was fourteen, while he was still studying in Vilna, his father, Rabbi Aryeh Leib HaKohen, a great Torah scholar, passed away. His mother married a widower businessman from the city of Radin and moved there with her new husband.

The Chafetz Chaim's stepfather had a daughter of marital age. When he heard that his new wife had an outstanding son in Vilna, he began to consider him as a possible husband for his daughter. He got to know Yisrael Meir, and they became close. Eventually Yisrael Meir agreed to meet the daughter, and they married.

The Chafetz Chaim was sixteen years old at the time. His father-in-law gave him a small house and supported the couple for several years. Rabbi Yisrael Meir sat at home and diligently studied Torah. A few short years after their marriage, his wife opened a grocery store which barely supported them. Because she had never learned how to write, Rabbi Yisrael Meir helped her in the evenings, when he returned from the *beis midrash*, to keep the daily accounts. He always spoke highly of his wife, because she was content to live simply and thus enable him to ascend the heights of Torah and work on his fear of God.

During his youth the Chafetz Chaim taught poor workers in the *beis midrash* in Radin. His primary topic was *Chayei Adam*, but he also spoke about fearing God and the holiness of the Torah. On Shabbos he taught them *Chumash* with *Rashi*. He also established a charity to lend money to people in need.

From when he was a young boy the Chafetz Chaim liked to spend time alone. Whether in the synagogue in Radin or on solitary walks, he would evaluate himself and his behavior each day. He kept a little pad in which he wrote down his self-evaluations. Most nights he slept in the *beis midrash*, where he kept two small pillows. The elders of Radin would tell the story of a poor bride on whose behalf the women of Radin collected feathers for pillows and covers for the bride. When the Chafetz Chaim heard about the collection, he donated his own pillows.

The Chafetz Chaim's method of studying Torah was to study in great depth. He would begin at the source of a given topic and study the subject all the way through to its practical halachic application. His son, the *gaon* Rabbi Leib, said that when he was fourteen he once studied the topic of the *eglah arufah* with his father. They started by studying the verses in the Torah with the *Sifri*, *Rashi*, and *Ramban*, as well as the Vilna Gaon's commentary. Then they studied the entire relevant chapter in the Mishnah with *Tosefta*. After that they turned to the discussion in *Talmud Bavli*, then in the *Yerushalmi*.

This was how the Chafetz Chaim wrote his *sefarim*. In the *Mishnah Berurah*, for example, he first discusses how the early *Rishonim* — the Rif, Rambam, the *Ba'alei HaTosafos*, and the Rosh — explain a topic and how they dealt with its practical applications. Then he discusses the opinions of the later *Rishonim* — the Semag, Or Zarua, Ramban, Rashba, Ritva, Ran, and Meiri. He did this to come to a clear understanding of the halachah.

When the Chafetz Chaim was thirty years old, he began to write his classic work *Chafetz Chaim*, which discusses the laws of speech. No one knows what inspired him to write this outstanding work. The Torah world was very excited when this book was published. Everyone who studied the *sefer* realized that Rabbi Yisrael Meir had been ordained by God to write this great work.

One of the Chafetz Chaim's concerns was that storeowners use correct weights and measures. He spoke publicly about the severe sin of cheating with improper scales, whether the customer is Jewish or not. After several years, he wrote a pamphlet on the subject. In his wife's store, not only did he keep close watch over the scales, but he also checked the foods that were sold to make sure they were fresh. Even so, he worried whether, God forbid, he had made a mistake, even if it involved a penny. He would contribute money to charity to make up for any mistake he may have unintentionally made.

In the summer of 5635 (1875), he began to write his major work, the *Mishnah Berurah* on *Orach Chaim*. Before he began to write it himself, he suggested to several great Torah scholars of his time that they write such a work, explaining the halachos fully and concluding with a definitive statement of the practical law on every topic. In the end, he undertook this difficult task himself. It took him twenty-eight years to complete.

THE OR YAHEL

Rabbi Yehudah Leib Chasman, the Or Yahel, was born in 5629 (1869), in Iva, a small village near Vilna. His father, Rephael, was a businessman and a devout Jew.

From an early age, Rabbi Yehudah Leib had outstanding faith in God and an excellent character. In his youth, he studied in the local *cheder* and *beis midrash* together with Chaim Ozer Grodzensky, also from Iva, who became one of the greatest *geonim* of his time. When Rabbi Yehudah Leib grew older, he went to Slobodka Yeshivah and studied under two great Torah scholars: Rabbi Yitzchak Blazer and Rabbi Nassan Tzvi Finkel, the *Alter* of Slobodka. In the poor synagogue called "The Funeral Procession Shul" and in the *"mussar shtibel,"* his appreciation for the study of *mussar* (ethics) ripened. He became known as one of the best students, serious and diligent in both Torah study and doing mitzvos.

In 5648 (1888) Rabbi Yehudah Leib traveled to the city of Kelm, a city of scholars and scribes. There he studied in the famous yeshivah of Kelm and quickly became one of the finest students of the *gaon* Rabbi Simchah Zissel. The *rav* was the founder of the yeshivah and the architect of the special Kelm approach to the study of *mussar*. Rabbi Yehudah Leib became very close to him, and Rabbi Simchah Zissel had great respect for him.

In 5649 (1889) Rabbi Avraham Yivnah, a respected merchant and devout Jew whose house and large sukkah served as a regular meeting place for the Torah scholars of Kelm, selected Yehudah Leib as a husband for his eldest daughter. On his wedding day, Yehudah Leib sat and studied in the *beis midrash*, as usual. Only when his in-laws came to tell him the time for the wedding ceremony had arrived did he get up. He returned home, dressed in his wedding clothes, and went to the ceremony.

His early married years were troubling years for Yehudah Leib. When he was a young *bachur* in Kelm, his entire life was wrapped up in the yeshivah. He was able to spend all his time with his rebbe, Rabbi Simchah Zissel. Now he was forced to spend most of his time working in the flour business in order to support his young family. Rabbi Yehudah Leib longed for his old life, when he was able to study with his colleagues and concentrate on his spiritual development.

In 5651 (1891), he finally left his business and family and traveled to Volozhin, where the Netziv lived. There he studied from the great masters of the famous Volozhin approach to Torah.

But Rabbi Yehudah Leib remained unsatisfied with his own level of knowledge. He yearned to study and know more. This great desire caused a fierce, unsettling spirit to stir within him, and he studied diligently to satisfy that desire.

In 5652 (1892), when the government forced Volozhin Yeshivah to close, Rabbi Yehudah Leib returned to Kelm and his business. But the thought of leaving his studies depressed him, so once again he left his home and family. This time he traveled to the faraway town of Lovtash, near Vilna, and studied Torah in the *beis midrash* day and night. In a letter he wrote to his young wife while in Lovtash, whom he had left alone and upon whom had fallen the burden of supporting their family and running the business, he encouraged her to withstand the situation, to understand that he was unable to do anything other than study Torah and that God's help can come in the blink of an eye. This simple, honest, and modest letter, and others like it, exhibited a great faith in God and are considered to be among the greatest letters written by a great Torah scholar.

Rabbi Yehudah Leib Chasman eventually became the *menahel ruchani* (spiritual leader) of the Chevron yeshivah Knesses Yisrael and the author of *Or Yahel*.

RABBI YEHUDAH PETIYA

Rabbi Yehudah Petiya was born in Baghdad on 2 Shevat 5619 (1859). His father, Rabbi Moshe, was a well-known Torah scholar and Kabbalist. Growing up in his father's home, Yehudah developed his spiritual roots, his thirst for Torah, and his kind personality.

As a child, Yehudah studied at Midrash Talmud Torah where his extraordinary intellect and his desire to conduct himself properly and learn Torah were evident. When he entered the yeshivah Beis Zilkah, he stood out with his exceptional understanding of the Talmud and Mishnah. His rebbe, Rabbi Abdallah Somach, had a special love for him. Rabbi Abdallah held Yehudah in such high regard that when Yehudah was just seventeen years old, Rabbi Abdallah gave him rabbinical ordination as both a teacher and a *poseik*.

Yehudah received his ordination when he and several other yeshivah students were staying in Rabbi Abdallah Somach's home. When it was time to daven *minchah*, Yehudah was asked to be the chazzan. One of the people present complained that according to the halachah a person is not supposed to the chazzan if he does not have a full beard. Rabbi Abdallah Somach got up and said firmly, "Are you saying that Yehudah cannot be the chazzan? You should know that he is a rare Torah scholar and that the only thing he is lacking is rabbinical ordination." Rabbi Abdallah then placed his hands on Yehudah's head and said, "I grant you ordination now as a rabbi. Everyone should now obey what Yehudah says as a rabbi and scholar of Yisrael."

Rabbi Yehudah began studying Kabbalah at a very young age. When he was just twenty-five years old, having studied Talmud and Mishnah, Yehudah authored his first holy work on Kabbalah, *Yayin HaRochach*. Later in life, he published other works, including *Masok LaNefesh*, *Minchas Yehudah*, *Chasdei David*, and his major work, *Beis Lechem Yehudah*.

As great as he was in Torah, he was always extremely humble. He tried to conceal his greatness and spirituality from others. But he became too well known, and people came to his door to obtain blessings and to be mentioned in his prayers.

RABBI ASHER ANSHEL KATZ

Rabbi Asher Anshel Katz was born on 18 Teves 5641 (1881) in the city of Teshenger. His father was Rabbi Yehonasan Binyamin Katz, a student of the Minchas Shai.

Before Rabbi Asher Anshel was born, his mother, Gitel, had miscarried several times. When she became pregnant with Asher Anshel, the *Gaon* of Kolmiya, author of *Maskil el Dal*, was in Teshenger and stayed at her father's home. She went to see the *Gaon* and told him her situation, how she so much wanted a child. She asked the *Gaon* to bless her that she would give birth to a healthy child. He told her not to worry — the child whom she would have would grow up to become a great Torah scholar. The blessing came true when she gave birth to Rabbi Asher Anshel Katz.

As a youngster Asher Anshel was sharp and diligent. He didn't spend much time playing games or with friends. He dedicated all his time to learning Torah. Later in life, he said that when he was eight years old he knew by heart the explanation of the Ran on a complex topic in *Chullin*.

Asher Anshel was modest about his good deeds. In Teshenger the mikveh was not heated every day, and therefore most people in the city did not immerse themselves daily, but Asher did. He would take a roundabout route, through courtyards and gardens, so no one would see where he was going.

When Asher was twelve, he traveled to Choset to study in the yeshivah of the Arugas HaBosem. He celebrated his bar mitzvah there and stayed on for eight years. Nine hours a day he would remain in his place, learning Torah without a break. After many years he earned the title "*rosh yeshivah*" — a title designated for the most outstanding student in the yeshivah.

Asher's greatness in Torah during his youth was demonstrated in an incident that occurred when Asher Anshel was just fourteen years old. He traveled from Choset to Spinka to spend time with Rabbi Yosef Meir, author of *Imrei Yosef*. By that time he knew all the laws of mikveh as explained in *Yoreh De'ah* and its commentaries. When he entered the room where the Rebbe was sitting, Asher found him surrounded by his followers, telling the following story.

When Rabbi Shalom, the head of the Belz *beis din*, sanctified the mikveh he built, he appointed watchmen to make sure that no one would touch the water in the mikveh until it filled up. But someone managed to approach the mikveh and touched the water before it had filled up. The watchmen immediately went to the rabbi and told him what had happened. The rabbi instructed them to empty the mikveh and resanctify it. Surprised at his stringent ruling, they went to Rabbi Shalom of Kaminika. The *gaon* also expressed his surprise — the halachah did not require that the whole mikveh be refilled. Later he said that he found the basis for the instruction to reconsecrate the mikveh in an obscure *Tosefta*.

When Asher Anshel heard this story he said, "The source of that halachah is not a *Tosefta*. It is expressly stated by the Shach in *Yoreh De'ah* (201:59) in the name of the Rambam."

Everyone present was amazed by this fourteen-year-old boy's knowledge. The Rebbe called him over and asked one of the men to give him a *Shulchan Aruch*. Asher Anshel showed the Rebbe the passage in the *Shach* exactly as he had quoted it. The great rabbi took Asher Anshel in his arms and kissed him on his forehead.

When he was older, Asher Anshel received rabbinical ordination from his rebbe, who told everyone of his student's greatness. He was also given *semichah* by the Maharsham, the *gaon* Rabbi Moshe Tzvi Fox, and the great rabbi known as the Levushei Mordechai. These distinguished Torah scholars praised Asher Anshel's greatness in Torah. Eventually Rabbi Asher Anshel became the head of the Sradahali *beis din* and wrote the responsa *U'LeAsher Amar*.

RABBI KALPON
MOSHE HAKOHEN

Rabbi Kalpon Moshe HaKohen, author of the responsa *Sho'el V'Nishal*, was born in Gorba on 12 Shevat 5634 (1874). At first, his father, the *gaon* Rabbi Shalom HaKohen taught him at home. When he grew a bit older, his father took him to Rabbi Yosef Birbi, author of *Yaldei Yosef* and *Bein Poras Yosef*. The *rav* had just been appointed chief rabbi of Gorba.

As a young child, Kalpon's brilliance shown through, and he advanced from class to class in a short time. His friends became jealous, because he got to study with the older children. But when they saw how smart, diligent, and quick he was, their jealousy turned into respect and genuine admiration.

Kalpon never wasted time. He would speak only *divrei Torah*. His friends honored his wishes and did not bother him unless it was to study Torah. Kalpon became well known throughout

Gorba as someone who would one day become a great *poseik*. His rebbe, Rabbi Yosef, also appreciated his greatness, so much so that he asked Kalpon to join in arranging a *chalitzah* ceremony for Rabbi Yosef's sister when the boy was still quite young. But Kalpon refused, reluctant to participate in a halachic ruling at so young an age.

When Kalpon prayed, he would say the words clearly and with great enthusiasm, as if each word were a valuable gem. When he was twelve, the great scholar Rabbi Shalom Chai Cohen, head of the Tchopochs *beis din* and author of *Tiferes Yisrael*, visited Gorba. In the synagogue he saw Kalpon praying with fierce concentration and intensity. Rabbi Shalom asked Rabbi Yaakov HaKohen about the boy. When Rabbi Yaakov told him the boy's family name, Rabbi Shalom said, "So it is. Future scholars are recognized by their youthful behavior." When he heard the boy discussing a Torah subject, he asked permission to take him back with him. He promised that Kalpon would have everything he needed. Kalpon's parents, however, would not let their son go.

Meanwhile, Kalpon's father was having a very difficult time earning a living. In this difficult situation, Kalpon continued to study with great diligence. When the situation worsened, though, Kalpon was forced to hire himself out to copy books to help his father support the family and to have enough money to purchase his own *sefarim*.

When Kalpon became seventeen, his father was appointed as a rabbi and teacher in the city of Zarzis. The community also suggested that Kalpon be appointed the *shochet* of the city. His father liked the idea, and Kalpon went to Rabbi Binya in Chadchad and Rabbi David Cohen to learn how to become a *shochet*. After he received his certificate he traveled to Zarzis and was appointed the *shochet* there.

Since the city was still developing, there was no slaughterhouse. Kalpon had to slaughter outside in the open air. It was summer and very hot. Day after day, the sun beat down on Kalpon as he labored. He came down with a terrible fever and was bedridden for several months. When his health improved, he regained his strength and was able to return to work. But his illness left him with a weak constitution. Still, he was determined to work hard in order to help support the family.

The rabbis of Gorba heard what had happened to their beloved student. They spoke to Kalpon's father, declaring that he was endangering the life of his son. Rabbi Moshe Edan wrote a very strong letter to Kalpon's father requesting that he send his son back to Gorba so he could continue his studies. Rabbi Shalom, notwithstanding his difficult financial situation, heeded the rabbis' request. But Kalpon's illness had affected his sight. Before he could return to Gorba, he was told to go to a certain highly regarded eye doctor in Malta for help.

Kalpon traveled with his mother to the island of Malta via Tripoli. They stayed with the pious rabbi and Kabbalist Rabbi Nissim Nachum. Kalpon and the rabbi became very close, and the young man told his family great things about the holiness and righteousness of Rabbi Nissim.

From Tripoli Kalpon traveled to Malta. The doctor there prescribed glasses and warned Kalpon not to study at night. At first, though he was generally very careful about his health, Kalpon did not follow the doctor's advice and learned Torah at night as well as during the day. In later years, he would study by having someone read to him and wrote long letters containing Torah discussions. Eventually he authored ten beautiful works.

RABBI MESHULAM IGRA

The great *tzaddik* Rabbi Meshulam Igra was the rabbi of Pressburg. Chassidim say that once Rabbi Yisrael Ba'al Shem Tov, the founder of Chassidus, was in the city of Botshut and noticed four-year-old Meshulam. The Ba'al Shem Tov looked at the child, then said to the people standing next to him, "Take a good look. Hashem gave this child a noble soul. There has not been a soul like this for many years."

Once Meshulam was sitting with several children reciting *pesukim* from *Chumash* for their rebbe. The rebbe listened to the children reciting the *pesukim*, which described Yosef's dream. In his dream, the sun, moon, and eleven stars bowed down to one star. The sun represents Yaakov, the moon represents Rachel, and the eleven stars represent Yosef's brothers bowing down to the one star, Yosef. The Torah says, "[Yosef's] father [Yaakov] was angry at him and said to him, 'What is this dream that you have dreamt? Will I, your mother, and your brothers bow down before you?' "

The children's teacher said to them, "Rashi explains that the moon in the dream represented Yosef's mother, Rachel. But his mother had already died. The Rabbis learn from this that every dream has some things in it that are not true."

Upon hearing this, young Meshulam jumped up and said, "Just because Yosef's dream had some things in it that were not true, must we say that *all* dreams have some things in it that are not true? Maybe his dream was the exception and not the rule."

All the children sat quietly, waiting for their rebbe to give an answer. But the teacher was also silent; he did not know how to answer the boy's question. Meshulam, though, did not stay silent. He thought for a few moments and then asked, "Why did Yosef say that he saw the moon in his dream? This made his father angry. His father thought that maybe the dream couldn't come true, since Rachel, whom the moon represented, was not alive. It would have been better if Yosef had left out that part of the dream when he told it to his father.

"I think," continued the child with sparkling eyes, "one question answers the other. Yosef did not skip anything when he told the dream, because he knew that every dream has something in it that is not true. If he had skipped the part about the moon, his father and brothers would have thought that the other parts of the dream were not true, since there has to be *something* that is not true. So he told them everything, even the part about the moon. From this our Rabbis learned that every dream contains something that is not true."

When he was just eight years old, Meshulam began to write explanations on the Torah. When he was nine, he understood most of the Talmud with both the earlier and later commentaries, and he became very well known. At the age of seventeen, the large Jewish community of Tizmintz, a city of Torah scholars and scribes, chose him to be their rabbi.

Rabbi Meshulam's diligence in Torah study was as great as his understanding and depth of knowledge. He literally never interrupted his studies.

Once Rabbi Meshulam was walking in the market of Tizmintz, thinking over a halachic matter, when he came across a wagon drawn by large, strong horses. The horses and wagon were going so fast that they knocked him down. Passersby ran quickly to rescue the rabbi. When they removed him from under the wagon, they heard him murmuring, "And according to this, the explanation of the Ravad on the Rambam is...." He had never interrupted his thoughts, immersed in halachah, even though he fell down and could have been seriously hurt!

RABBI YOSEF TZVI DUSHINSKY

Rabbi Yosef Tzvi Dushinsky was born on 25 Tamuz 5627 (1867) in the town of Paks. His father, Rabbi Yisrael, saw the year of Rabbi Yosef Tzvi's birth, which in Hebrew spells out the word *zechor*, "remember," as a good omen: "The child will have a good memory and a sharp mind."

And so it was. Yosef Tzvi's talents were apparent from the moment his father started teaching him alef-beis. He quickly grasped everything he was taught.

Rabbi Yisrael enrolled his son in the local yeshivah, the only school in the area. Students even traveled from the capital city, Pest, to study there for lack of another school. Rabbi Yosef Erengruberger was the rebbe there, and he soon recognized young Yosef Tzvi Dushinsky's natural diligence and intelligence.

Yosef did not spend much time with the other children; he was hardly ever seen playing games with them. He spent his free time reviewing his studies. His rebbe marveled over Yosef Tzvi's willingness to help other children who did not understand what they were learning. Patiently, he would explain the lessons to them over and over.

Prayer was very important to Yosef Tzvi. He found an inconspicuous corner in the shul where he could quietly recite *tehillim*. Sometimes someone would notice the little boy crying in a corner. Concerned he would ask, "Why are you crying, child?" Yosef Tzvi would explain, with a sweet innocence, "I am crying before the Almighty, pleading that He give me the ability to understand His Torah."

Once, Yosef Tzvi's father found him alone in shul reciting *tehillim* in a sweet, melodious tone. Surprised, his father asked, "Why are you reciting *tehillim*, my son?"

"I saw that people say *tehillim* in shul," answered Yosef Tzvi, "and I said to myself that this is a good custom." Those who saw him pray during those early years said that he prayed regularly, day in and day out, crying to the Almighty.

Yosef Tzvi's enormous diligence and extensive knowledge of Mishnah were the talk of the city. His father, an experienced teacher at the local elementary school, understood the value of his gifted son. He put a lot of effort into increasing his son's knowledge.

Yosef Tzvi himself had a great desire to increase his proficiency in Torah. The place where he was studying was too limited for his needs. When his older brother went to the yeshivah of the Maharam Schick in 5638 (1878) he, too, wanted to go. But Hashem had other plans — the Maharam Schick passed away in the beginning of 5639 (1879). Throughout his life Rabbi Yosef Tzvi regretted that he never heard Torah from the Maharam Schick, though he studied his commentary on his own.

As the year 5640 (1880) approached, Rabbi Yosef Tzvi entered the yeshivah in Banihad, which in a short time became a leading institution in the area. Yosef Tzvi filled every moment of his day with Torah and serving God. Like the other students, he ate at people's homes, but always he brought with him a *sefer*, *Akeidah*, which he studied during the brief moments between courses. He completed the *sefer* just from those few minutes of learning it each day. His study of *Akeidah* was his example of how one can do so much by utilizing every moment.

Later in life, Yosef Tzvi would tell over an incident that occurred to him to show how much use he made of every free moment. Once, he went to visit a sick friend and told him how important it was to take care of himself. He reminded his friend, "When we were young, we studied late into the night. In the mornings we were among the first in the *beis midrash*. We'd skip a few stairs at a time in our rush to get to the *beis midrash* more quickly, not wishing to waste a moment."

Though Yosef Tzvi spent all his time studying Torah, he was not wealthy, to say the least. His father was unable to support him. Often, Yosef Tzvi had no idea where he would get the few coins he needed just to live. His poverty forced him to live on a careful budget, and he frequently skipped meals because he did not have any money. Once he told his younger brother, "At first we ate two meals each day for our health. Later we decided to eat lunch just twice a week with the few coins we had in our pockets so we would have the strength to study Torah. Once I felt very weak. So as not to miss a learning session I decided to eat lunch every day. In two weeks I had no money. Since I didn't have another choice at that point, I spent the money that had been set aside for travel expenses. Then, completely unexpectedly, I received money from another source which lasted for a month. I undertook to sleep an hour less each day and study Torah with more energy in gratitude to Hashem for His kindness to me."

The meals in yeshivos in those days were usually quite skimpy and did not satisfy the boys' hunger. When the students complained about the nutritional conditions in the yeshivah in Khust, Rabbi Yosef Tzvi responded, "When we studied with Rabbi Zekel, our Shabbos meal consisted of bread and a handful of nuts — and we were happy to receive such 'delicacies.' "

Yosef Tzvi had a compassionate heart. Anyone who knew him never forgot how he prayed, with tears running down his face. His friends were amazed by his devotion and by the intensity with which he davened. They even gave him a special *shtender* at which to pray.

Once, Rabbi Akiva Yosef Shlesinger came to the yeshivah when he left Eretz Yisrael in 5644 (1884) to visit the graves of his ancestors. The great rabbi saw Yosef Tzvi praying with intensity, his body swaying back and forth while he recited the words. He approached Yosef Tzvi, amazed at how a person could be so physically involved in his prayers, and remarked, "Don't change the way you pray. It is appropriate for you."

In 5645 (1885), when Yosef Tzvi was eighteen, he moved to the yeshivah in Pressburg. Mordechai Eliezer Erengruberger, his childhood friend who later became a great Torah scholar and the head of the *beis din* in Veravov, went with him. When they left their parents' homes, all the great rabbis and leaders of Paks came out to see them off at the docks as a symbol of the esteem in which they held these great young Torah scholars, the pride of the city. It was a spectacular event which demonstrated the great love of Torah which burned in the hearts of the citizens of this community.

Within several weeks in Pressburg, Yosef Tzvi was recognized as one of the best students in the yeshivah. On Shabbos of *parashas Vayishlach* he was asked to deliver a Torah discourse for a study group called Tiferes Shabbos. After a while, he organized a group of young men with whom he would review the lectures of his rebbe. When this group was tested, their rebbe complimented them on their knowledge of the lecture material.

Yosef Tzvi's diligence stood out among the hundreds of students in the yeshivah. He was never among the first to enter the dining room, but by the time the first shift of students had left, he had managed to learn some Tanach or *aggadah*. When he himself was a rebbe, he would emphasize to his students how important every moment is. He would tell them that he had learned many important lessons waiting in line to enter the dining room.

Rabbi Yosef Tzvi Dushinsky became the head of the *beis din* in Jerusalem and the chief rabbi of the Eidah Chareidis in Israel.

RABBI BEN TZION MEIR CHAI UZIEL

Rabbi Ben Tzion Meir Chai Uziel, the Rishon L'Tzion and chief rabbi of Israel, was born in Jerusalem on 13 Sivan 5640 (1880). His father was Rabbi Yosef Rephael Uziel, head of the *beis din* of Jerusalem. His mother, Sarah, was the daughter of Rabbi Moshe Chazzan. Her great-grandfather, Rabbi Yosef Rephael Chazzan, was the author of the well-known twelve-volume *Chakrei Lev*. Rabbi Chaim David Chazzan, Sarah's grandfather, was a well-known scholar who was nicknamed "Rabbi Chad Badra," a play on words using the letters of his name. It means "one of a kind in his time." Both father and son were appointed as chief rabbis with the title Rishon L'Tzion.

Ben Tzion Meir Chai Uziel studied Torah with his father and many other great scholars at the famous Tiferes Yerushalayim Yeshivah in the Old City of Jerusalem. His primary teacher was Rabbi Ben Tzion Koinka, a great Torah scholar and the editor of *HaMarech* and author of several important works on halachah.

Though he had excellent teachers, Ben Tzion Meir acquired much of his Torah knowledge through independent study. It was difficult for him to learn with his peers, because his grasp was so fast and sharp that he could not get used to the slower pace at which his friends studied.

In 5654 (1894), at the age of fourteen, Ben Tzion Meir's father passed away. As the oldest child, the responsibility for supporting the family fell on his young shoulders. His diligence and intelligence stood him well in these difficult times.

Ben Tzion Meir became well known in halachic circles as a scholar with extraordinary potential and abilities. In 5660 (1900), when he was a mere twenty years old, he was appointed as a rebbe in Tiferes Yerushalayim.

During the next twelve years Rabbi Ben Tzion Meir assumed important positions in the community, in addition to being a respected Torah scholar. He was one of the founders of the School for Orphans and established the yeshivah Machzikei Torah, whose purpose was to produce rabbis for the Sephardic community. He had a reputation as a gifted speaker and an active and successful community leader.

In 5672 (1912), when he was thirty-two years old, Rabbi Ben Tzion Meir was appointed chief rabbi of the Tel Aviv–Jaffa area. He gave his inauguration speech, which was comprised of both a deep halachic discussion as well as a moving presentation of *aggadah*, in the Kehilas Yaakov synagogue in Jaffa on 6 Cheshvan 5672.

On 10 Tamuz 5697 (1937), Rabbi Ben Tzion moved to Jerusalem to serve as chief rabbi of Israel and the Rishon L'Tzion. Crowds of Tel Aviv residents assembled to bid him a bittersweet farewell that morning. And in Jerusalem, crowds of Jerusalem residents came out to greet the new chief rabbi at the entrance to the city.

THE CHAZON ISH

Rabbi Avraham Yeshayahu Karelitz was born on 11 Cheshvan 5639 (1879). His father was Rabbi Shemaryahu Yosef; his mother, the saintly Raasha Leah. His parents, particularly his mother, decided to dedicate their son entirely to the spiritual. Everything they did was intended to add to his holiness. From the day he was born, they were careful to always cover his head with a yarmulke woven by his mother. When he was thirty days old, his mother began washing his hands every morning to remove the *tumah* that stays on the hands from the nighttime. When he began to talk and understand what he was told, she taught him *birkas haTorah*, several selected verses, and the alef-beis.

Avraham Yeshayahu was a smart boy, and he had a pleasant way about him. Anyone who met him came away impressed by his brilliance. When he was three years old, he surprised his father one day when he said, "I am an expert in the entire Talmud!"

"How did that happen?" asked his amazed father.

The child explained, "Go ahead! Find me a single letter of

the alef-beis in the Talmud that I do not recognize!"

The extraordinary intellectual abilities of young Avraham Yeshayahu, who showed a special interest in intensive Torah study, surprised his rebbe. The time came when the rebbe felt he had nothing more to teach the young prodigy. The rebbe approached Avraham Yeshayahu's father and mother and told them that their son needed a new teacher. Rabbi Shemaryahu Yosef decided to set aside time each day to teach Avraham Yeshayahu Gemara. The rest of the day Avraham Yeshayahu studied by himself in Beis Midrash HaYashan in Kosov. He didn't attend one of the famous yeshivos, as was the custom in those days. Instead, he acquired his vast Torah knowledge through independent study, guided by his father's teachings and approach, his father being a faithful follower of the Vilna Gaon's teachings.

"*Nu*, if you have to figure out a difficult halachah, you stay up all night until you figure it out!" — a famous saying of the Chazon Ish in his later years, intoned while humming a tune. During his youth he lived up to this principle. Many times he stayed up all night studying. His loving mother, Rebbetzin Raasha Leah, worried that he was ruining his health, would rebuke him for not getting enough sleep. Avraham Yeshayahu came up with ways to fool his mother into thinking that he had really slept in his bed. He'd prepare a small kerosene lamp which he covered with sheets and blankets so that the light would only hit his table and spread no further. Leaning over his books in the darkness of the night, he would study under that small light. His mother thought he was obeying her and sleeping all night peacefully, until she found out that Avraham Yeshayahu had been up studying all those times.

Avraham Yeshayahu did not play or cause mischief like the other children. He loved to study Torah and devoted all his time to it. From early childhood Avraham Yehsayahu always went to the *beis midrash* with one thing in mind: "Be diligent in Torah study! Study very hard, with unlimited effort, and with everything you have, because Torah is our life." His greatest desire was to dedicate all the years of his life completely to the Almighty and to the study of Torah.

When he became bar mitzvah, obligated to perform all the mitzvos, he delivered his bar mitzvah speech in front of the scholars and leaders of Kosbah, who came to his father's home to hear him. In his speech, he promised, "I will learn Torah for the sake of Heaven all the days of my life." And so he did.

RABBI EFRAIM HAKOHEN

Rabbi Efraim HaKohen was the head of the Kabbalah scholars in Porat Yosef Yeshivah. He was born in Baghdad in 5645 (1885) and studied in that city's yeshivos. When he was eighteen, he began to learn Kabbalah by himself. When Rabbi Shimon Agasi, a great *talmid chacham*, found out, he told Rabbi Efraim, "Stop studying Kabbalah — you will not be able to do it by yourself." Rabbi Efraim told him, "Do you know how much I've studied already?" Rabbi Agasi tested Efraim and realized that he was a fount of knowledge — Efraim never forgot anything he studied and fully understood everything he learned. Rabbi Agasi looked at him with new respect and began learning with Rabbi Efraim several nights a week. They studied together for six years.

When he was a young boy, Efraim formed a special relationship with Rabbi Yosef Chaim, the Ben Ish Chai, who was among Efraim's greatest admirers and supporters. So high was his opinion of Efraim that the Ben Ish Chai said to him, "Come to me any time. I've told my household that even if I'm sleeping when you come, they should wake me." Efraim visited the *rav*'s home often to discuss Torah and get advice.

Because Efraim's parents were very poor, the family was forced to move to another city, hoping to earn a better living. Efraim faced a dilemma: the city to which they were moving had no *beis midrash* or scholars from whom to learn, but if he stayed in Baghdad, how would he support himself? The few pennies he received from the *beis midrash* were not enough to live on.

As he always did when he sought advice, he went to the Ben Ish Chai. His mentor told him, "Do not go with them. Hashem will help."

Efraim followed his rebbe's advice. His financial condition was extremely difficult, and he reached a point where he was ready to give up. But he refused to ask for charity, and no one knew how bad his situation had become. It was during this time that the Ben Ish Chai passed away. In the midst of his crisis, Efraim cried out to his beloved rebbe in prayer: "Rabbi Yosef Chaim! You advised me to go on the path which I have chosen, and I did so. Now see the difficult situation in which I find myself. I cannot pray by your grave because I am a *kohen*. I ask now that you pray for me so I will be saved." The next afternoon, he received a telegram from his parents: "We are returning home."

In 5684 (1924) Efraim moved to Jerusalem, fulfilling his life-long dream. When he left Baghdad, many people, including many of the city's scholars, came to see him off. Tears ran down faces and hearts were heavy at bidding farewell to such a great *talmid chacham*.

When Efraim arrived in Jerusalem, he decided to learn in the Kabbalah yeshivah Porat Yosef. There he studied with the *gaon* Rabbi Chaim Shaul Dweck HaKohen. He excelled in his studies and earned the title "Elder of the Kabbalists."

Throughout his life Rabbi Efraim fasted frequently and denied himself simple pleasures to bring forgiveness for the Jewish people and to hasten the coming of the final redemption. His was an extraordinary life of spirituality.

RABBI RACHAMIM CHAI CHAVITAH HAKOHEN

In the city of Gorba, on Shabbos 22 Sivan 5661 (1901), Rabbi Rachamim Chai Chavitah HaKohen was born. His father, Rabbi Chanina, found it difficult to support his family, but he never asked his son to help him in his work. "Study hard," he would tell Rachamim. "Torah is more valuable than gold and jewels." Rachamim was an obedient child, and he studied diligently.

Rachamim's teachers recognized that the child was destined for greatness. He studied with an intensity that showed how much he loved Torah. He'd review his studies, again and again, late into the night. When he realized that his father always waited up for him, he would close his book, go to his room, and pretend he was going to sleep. Exhausted from working all day, his father would finally go to bed and would fall into a deep sleep. Then Rachamim would get up, light the lamp, and learn for hours without interruption.

When he was fifteen, he learned the principles of making halachic decisions from Rabbi Moshe Kalpon, the author of the *Sho'el V'Nishal*. By that time Rachamim had already begun to correspond with the great Torah scholars of the time on halachic questions and responsa. After a number of years he received ordination as a *shochet* and served as a *sofer* for the Gorba *beis din*.

When Rachamim was twenty years old, he began to teach Torah. His students loved him intensely, and he, in turn, spent many hours each day on their behalf. He looked after their needs and was concerned with their development. He trained them to compose original Torah insights on the Talmud and *Chumash*. Then he would edit and improve them. His care and encouragement made them love studying Torah even more.

Rachamim liked to teach no more than twenty-five students at a time. He was concerned that any more students than that would diminish the quality of the students' education. Parents made sure to enroll their children way in advance to ensure a place in his class.

Rachamim often did not take time to eat when he was teaching, so involved did he get in what he was doing. Once, his students put a plate of delicious-looking black grapes on his table for him to eat. But all of Rabbi Rachamim's attention was on the lesson he was giving. He was concentrating so hard that as he took each grape he dipped it in salt and then plopped it in his mouth. The plate of grapes were finished, and he never noticed the strange flavor.

RABBI AKIVA SOFER

Rabbi Akiva Sofer, head of the Pressburg *beis din* in Pressburg and the author of *Da'as Sofer*, was born in Pressburg in 5638 (1878). His father was a *talmid chacham*, known as the Shevet Sofer, after the *sefer* he wrote. Akiva learned in his father's yeshivah, and with his enormous intellect Akiva was able, even as a child, to advance a great deal in Torah. He quickly became known as one of the finest students in the yeshivah, an institution where all three hundred students were considered exceptional.

Akiva was a very intense student — each moment was valuable to him, and he did not waste time. Akiva used to tell a story of how his father told him not to waste a minute. His father recommended that he study the laws of *shechitah* during recess. Akiva took his father's advice and at fourteen received his certification as a *shochet* from Rabbi Amram Kurtzweil, the city *shochet*.

When Akiva turned twenty, he began teaching the advanced classes of the yeshivah with his father. Thanks to his prowess in

Torah and his amazing memory, he became well known for his sharp insights, his depth of understanding, and clear logic. His breadth of knowledge was extraordinary as well: he composed insights on the most complex Talmudic topics of halachah and originated beautiful expositions on *aggadah*.

Akiva taught Torah with his father until 5667 (1907), when his father passed away. At the funeral, the Torah scholars who were present announced Akiva's appointment as his father's successor. His uncle Rabbi Shlomo Sofer, head of the Aragsaz *beis din* and author of *Chut HaMeshulash*, delivered a long and moving eulogy for his brother. At the end, he blessed his deceased brother, the Shevet Sofer; his nephew, the young *gaon* Rabbi Akiva; and the entire community on the occasion of Akiva's ascension to the rabbinate. Everyone responded, "Long live our master, teacher, and rabbi!" With great emotion Akiva stood up, and everyone cried with him as he gave an extraordinary, moving eulogy for his father.

After the *shivah*, Akiva's inauguration ceremony was held. A huge crowd filled the large synagogue, and Akiva was officially appointed the head of the *beis din* and *rosh hayeshivah*. In his address, Akiva made his famous comment (quoting from Selichos), " 'I believe in these' — honest people — and 'in the merit of the three forefathers,' the Chasam Sofer, the Kesav Sofer, and the Shevet Sofer, the Almighty will assist me to fulfill my responsibilities properly." When he finished his speech, Rabbi Leib Friedman approached him and kissed his hand. At twenty-nine Akiva had been appointed to follow his father's footsteps as the fourth generation in his family to serve as the rabbi of Pressburg.

After his appointment, Akiva went to visit the great Rabbi David Lekanbach, head of the *beis din*. Though Reb David was old and weak, an invalid, he got up the strength to rise from his bed when Akiva entered his room and, his eyes raised toward Heaven, said, "*Baruch Hashem*, the future generations are assured." The elderly *gaon* took out a bottle of wine and preceded his blessing over the wine with the words "in honor of our teacher and rabbi." Soon after, Rabbi Akiva published his father's *sefer Shevet Sofer*, a commentary on the four sections of the *Shulchan Aruch*. It appeared in print in 5669 (1909).

Rabbi Akiva enthusiastically became involved in all aspects of Torah and Jewish community affairs. As the head of the *beis din* and rabbi of Pressburg, he undertook many projects to improve the community. People listened to him without hesitation. With his larger-than-life personality, he was able to influence many different types of groups, all of whom valued and respected him. The community began to develop with great speed. The city's existing institutions grew larger and became more successful. Rabbi Akiva's influence could be seen everywhere, and his reputation spread all over the country. The young *gaon*, who had ascended to the rabbinical position of both his father and grandfather, became well known and respected in his own right by the elder Torah scholars of his generation.

RABBI YAAKOV GEDALYAHU WALDENBURG

Rabbi Yaakov Gedalyahu Waldenburg was born in Kovna. His parents were God-fearing and raised their son on a solid foundation of Torah. Wishing him to have a strong Torah education, they sent him to the best Lithuanian yeshivos.

True to his name, Yaakov had a propensity for the truth, as did Yaakov Avinu, and the ability to think clearly. These traits contributed to his basic approach to faith and study. He learned to be decisive, that even though indecision may at first appear to be a good approach, it leads to bad results. Yaakov chose the path of Godliness, which brings a person to the ultimate realization that God is before man at all times showing him the road of eternal light. As a result, Yaakov always thought before he spoke, and his worldly outlook was bright and clear, never superficial. He served his Creator with his whole heart and felt that Torah study and mitzvos were primary.

Because of his faith and deep understanding, he was compelled to dedicate himself to studying Torah and serving God faithfully. Some boys his age sought fulfillment in the secular world, but he was not swayed to follow them. To them he would quote his favorite verse, "And I anointed my King on Tzion, the holy mountain."

Eventually Yaakov traveled to Israel to study. When he arrived, he went straight from the port in Jaffa to visit the *gaon* Rabbi Yosef Tzvi HaLevi, who was from his hometown, and to meet the leaders of the city. They recognized that before them stood a young man with great potential and tried to convince Yaakov to establish his home in their city. They promised to take care of all his spiritual and worldly needs. But Yaakov's mind was set. He was determined to make his home in Jerusalem.

In Jerusalem, Yaakov immediately began to work toward the fulfillment of his life's vision. He entered the famous yeshivah Toras Chaim. Those who studied with Yaakov there remember with awe his dedication to learning.

Yaakov's first home in Jerusalem was the house of Rabbi Pesach Tzvi Frank, who also came from Kovno. Rabbi Frank and his *rebbetzin* welcomed him with outstretched arms and warmth. They cared for his every need. When Rabbi Frank saw that this young man had the wisdom of a more mature man, and that Yaakov was a diligent student of Torah, Rabbi Frank decided that he would make a good son-in-law for the *tzaddik* Rabbi Nachum Rogznitzky. The other *chachamim* he consulted agreed with him, and Rabbi Frank brought Yaakov before the chief rabbi of Jerusalem, Rabbi Shmuel Salant, to be tested. Yaakov completed his test successfully, and Rabbi Frank called Yaakov's father to tell him of this young man?" said Rabbi Frank to Rabbi Rogznitzky when everything was settled. "Take him and sanctify him." This is how the marriage came to fruition, much to the joy of the scholars and Torah students of Jerusalem.

Immediately after the wedding, Yaakov, at his father-in-law's request, went to study and teach in Yeshivas Eitz Chaim. The ability to focus and think logically was just as apparent there as it had been in all the other places he had studied. He found serenity in his studies and never tired of it. For hours he would stand at his *shtender*, studying out loud. His explanations were so clear and convincing that students were drawn to him, eager to learn from him.

Yaakov prayed the way he studied — intense, free of any impure thought. He would say each word out loud as if he were counting valuable pearls, and the words emanated from the depths of his heart. It was evident from the creases on his forehead and the general seriousness that enveloped him that he was standing before the King of kings as a servant stands before his master — with fear and awe, with songs of praise and the desire to do His will. His pronunciation was perfect, his speech clear and pleasant.

Yaakov's devotion was especially great when he recited "*Ahavah Rabbah*." He was full of thanks to the Almighty for giving the Jewish people the Torah, and his entire being was full of praise that God placed in the hearts of all Jews the ability to understand and be illuminated by the words of His Torah. When he reached the Shema, he would concentrate fully on accepting the yoke of God's kingship. Those who prayed with him trembled when they heard him recite the words that declared his acceptance of God's sovereignty.

Rabbi Yaakov merited to have a son who became a *talmid chacham* in his own right: Rabbi Eliezer Yehudah Waldenburg, a member of the *beis din hagadol* of Jerusalem and author of *Tzitz Eliezer*.

RABBI YISRAEL ZEV MINZBURG

Rabbi Yisrael Zev Minzburg was born on 14 Elul 5632 (1872), in Turbin, Poland. Five years later, his father, Rabbi Moshe Tzvi, immigrated to Israel. After a year, Yisrael Zev and his sister came to Israel with their mother, Golda.

When Yisrael Zev was a bar mitzvah, his uncle Rabbi Yerachmiel Yeshayah Minzburg predicted that the boy would "grow into a great tree," an analogy for a *tzaddik*, who produces mitzvos like fruit. Yisrael Zev loved to study and developed a reputation as one of the greatest young scholars of his time.

Sadly, Yisrael Zev's mother passed away when he was a child. He moved in with his grandfather, Rabbi Avraham Eliezer, who became his rebbe. Most of the Torah knowledge he gained as a child came from his grandfather, who inspired Yisrael Zev with his greatness and broad knowledge.

Yisrael Zev was a good-natured child, pleasant and friendly. He avoided disagreements at all costs and would not even support a political party because he believed they were a source of contention.

From his youth, he would discuss Torah subjects with the great Torah scholars of his day, including Rabbi Shneur Zalman of Lublin, the author of *Toras Chesed*, and Rabbi Yehoshua Leib Diskin. The Maharsha Alfandri loved him very much and asked that he visit him weekly for several hours to discuss halachah and his original Torah thoughts. The *gaon* used to say that Yisrael Zev's Torah insights were excellent and true.

Gaining the correct understanding of halachah was Yisrael Zev's focus. Since he was blessed with a clear intellect, he was able to make halachic decisions. In this capacity he served his people. They came to him from all over with their halachic questions, among them great Torah scholars. Yisrael Zev answered each question succinctly and became known as someone who illuminated the world with the light of Torah.

Rabbi Yisrael Zev became the head of the *beis din* of the Chassidic community of Jerusalem and wrote *She'eiris Yisrael*.

RABBI AVRAHAM SHMUEL BINYAMIN SOFER

Rabbi Avraham Shmuel Binyamin Sofer was the head of the Pressburg *beis din* and the author of *Chashav Sofer*. He was born on the first day of Marcheshvan 5662 (1902) to the *gaon* Rabbi Akiva Sofer, who wrote *Da'as Sofer* and was an inspiration to Avraham.

Avraham's dedication to Torah study, his intensity in serving God, and his exceptional intellectual abilities all contributed to his impressive reputation. He was praised as having a precise, analytical mind and an authentic knowledge of Torah.

Avraham learned under the influence of his father, the Da'as Sofer. His sole desire was to be as knowledgeable and God-fearing as his father. And Avraham did, indeed, merit to ascend the heights of both Torah knowledge and fear of God.

Avraham rented a separate room for himself — since he studied late into the night, he was concerned that he would disturb his parents' sleep and be forced to adjust his routine. This way he ensured that nothing interfered with his ascent in the service of God.

At the age of twenty-three, Avraham was appointed *rosh yeshivah* of Pressburg. He gave regular lectures to hundreds of outstanding students, utilizing the clear approach of the Chasam Sofer. This involved delving deeply into a topic, explaining it with an analysis of both the early and later commentaries. Avraham added his own precise insights, based on his expansive knowledge. His lectures became famous throughout Europe.

During these years, Avraham studied Torah diligently. He wrote down many notebooks' worth of original ideas on page after page of the Talmud. For eighteen years he went on this way until, in 5703 (1943), in the height of World War II, the Jewish communities in Slovakia, including Pressburg, were destroyed.

All his life Avraham looked for precise interpretations of the halachah. He also merited to teach Torah to many students over a period of thirty-six years and to see the fruits of his labor: his disciples became the pride of the Jewish people. But he was not satisfied. Additionally, Avraham tried with all his ability to improve the material circumstances of Torah students. He was devoted to seeing to his students' needs so they would be able to study Torah without worry.

RABBI OVADIAH HADAYAH

The *gaon* and Kabbalist Rabbi Ovadiah Hadayah, born in Syria in 5650 (1890), was the author of *Yaskil Avdi*. His father, Rabbi Shalom Hadayah, was a prominent scholar and the author of many *sefarim* on halachah and *aggadah*; he later became a head of the Jerusalem *beis din*. His maternal grandfather was Rabbi Yitzchak Labbaton, a member of the Jerusalem *beis din*, who came from a family of scholars and scribes. Rabbi Yitzchak's grandfather was the great Torah scholar Rabbi Mordechai Labbaton, the chief rabbi of Aram Soba and the author of *Nochach HaShulchan*.

When Ovadiah was five years old, his family emigrated to Jerusalem. Like the other boys there he was educated in Doresh Tzion, an elementary school. Then he attended Chesed Avraham yeshivah and after that Tiferes Yerushalayim.

Ovadiah was a challenging student for his teachers. His father recognized his son's potential and wanted to hire an expert teacher who would teach Ovadiah the proper approach in Talmudic study. He selected Rabbi Shalom Bochbot, a pious Jew and a great Kabbalist. This saintly man prayed according to the dictates of the Ari and studied Torah all day. Rabbi Shalom Hadayah knew that Rabbi Bochbot was very poor, so he promised to compensate him well if he would teach his son for a month on a trial basis. Ovadiah and Rabbi Bochbot developed a close relationship, and Ovadiah began his studies in Kabbalah with him. He was only seventeen years old, an extraordinarily young age to begin learning Kabbalah.

The elders of the city knew that a lovely seedling was blossoming in Rabbi Shalom's home, one that would ultimately become a beautiful vine in *klal Yisrael*'s vineyard. Ovadiah studied day and night in the *beis midrash*. He was like a well of knowledge that never lost a drop. He was never satisfied with his accomplishments — he pushed himself to study and ascend to higher and higher levels. He exemplified the dictum "He who has a hundred wants two hundred," but whereas Chazal applied it to money and physical objects, he applied it to his spiritual life. The Torah he studied at the expense of his physical well-being made a permanent impression on his soul and was absorbed into his every fiber.

It was common to find Ovadiah leaning over his books until late at night. His father, concerned for the boy's health, begged him to go to bed. Ovadiah would dim the light in his room, and after his father fell asleep, he would return to his studies until dawn. In this way, the verse "And all the nations of the land will see that the name of God is inscribed upon you, and they will fear you" was fulfilled by him: the Arab watchman who kept watch in the courtyard at night told of his amazement that Ovadiah kept his light on all night — and scared any thieves away.

Ovadiah's other teachers, besides his father, were Rabbi Yitzchak Sarim and Rabbi Yitzchak Alfiya. Ovadiah's studies were multifaceted — he did not restrict himself to the study of a particular tractate. He studied *Chumash*, Mishnah, and both the Babylonian and Jerusalem Talmud. He learned halachah, *aggadah*, and Kabbalah. His knowledge of Mishnah was truly extraordinary — he learned eighteen chapters of Mishnah a day.

Ovadiah started giving regular lectures in a synagogue in the Ohel Moshe neighborhood to the members of the Shomrim LaBoker study group. The city's *gedolim* respected him, and he was treated like a member of the family by the Sephardic chief rabbi. He also became friendly with Rabbi Ben Tzion Koinka, the author of *Me'aseif*.

Ovadiah would go to the Kabbalah yeshivah Beis El, in the heart of Jerusalem's Sephardic community. When he was a teenager, he would watch closely the saintly Kabbalist Rabbi Sasson Bechar Moshe, the author of *Shemen Sasson* and a chazzan in Beis El Yeshivah.

Ovadiah studied the expressions and mannerisms of the Kabbalists when they prayed, utilizing the meditations of the Ari and his disciples. Their obvious contentment made a deep impression on Ovadiah. It was then that he decided to cling to these great men, and his soul yearned to delve into Kabbalah.

Eventually Rabbi Ovadiah was chosen to be one of the teachers in the yeshivah. He studied Kabbalah day and night and became known as a great scholar in both traditional Torah study and Kabbalah.

RABBI EZRA ATAYA

Rabbi Ezra Ataya, *rosh yeshivah* of Porat Yosef in Jerusalem, was born on 16 Shevat. His father was Rabbi Yitzchak Ataya, a teacher of young children. His mother, Leah, was the daughter of Rabbi Michael Shema, a descendant of Rabbi Eliyahu Shema, the author of *Karbon Ishea*.

When Ezra was three years old, he attended a *cheder* for children of Syrian descent. When he began to study with Rabbi Eliyahu Aboud, a famous teacher at that time, it became clear that Ezra was at a higher level than the other children.

His parents were extremely pleased, but they were also concerned. Who could teach their precious jewel? They found Rabbi Yehudah Ataya, a righteous man with a stunning character. He gave Ezra, his beloved student, a foundation with which to delve deeply into the Torah. Ezra also had an excellent study partner, Shaul Matlov Abbadi, the grandson of Rabbi Mordechai Abbadi. Shaul had a sharp mind and was extremely serious about his studies.

Ezra's dedication and diligence paid off. His command of the Talmud and its commentaries was awesome, and he also acquired an expansive knowledge of the *Shulchan Aruch* and its commentaries. But he was modest about his accomplishments, and no one yet recognized his greatness.

The year 5666 (1906) was pivotal in the life of the Ataya family. Ezra's father, Rabbi Yitzchak, could not cope with the pressures of supporting his family, and he became ill. On the fifteenth of Marcheshvan he passed away. The despair of losing his father affected Ezra terribly. His older brother and sister were already married, and the responsibility for caring for his mother rested on him.

The Atayas went through a difficult time, and Ezra and his mother went hungry. The boy was not concerned with his own welfare; he accepted the pains of hunger. But Ezra could not stand to see his mother's pain when an *erev Shabbos* arrived and there was not a penny in the house with which to prepare for Shabbos. He walked around the empty house, hoping to find something he could sell.

"Why aren't you going to study in the *beis midrash*?" his mother asked.

"How can I go when I do not have a thing to give you?" Ezra responded.

"Don't worry," his mother told him firmly. "Your job is to study Torah. Hashem will help us."

Ezra went off to the *beis midrash*. He was able to forget his troubles when he was learning, but Shabbos was approaching and it was time to return home. As he entered the house, his mother greeted him with a glowing face. A surprise awaited him. They had everything they needed for Shabbos! With a bright smile, his mother told Ezra how it happened.

"I found an old gold earring which I received when I became engaged. I had forgotten all about it. I sold it in honor of Shabbos."

The days passed. His mother looked for work, even back-breaking jobs, to support herself and Ezra. But she did not succeed, and there was no alternative — Ezra decided to get a job just so they would have money to buy food.

At that time a Syrian yeshivah opened in Jerusalem. Rabbi Ezra Harrari Rafuel was instrumental in establishing the yeshivah, and Rabbi Shlomo Laniado became its head. When Rabbi Harrari Rafuel heard that Ezra had begun to learn carpentry from his uncle he was shocked. *Will the world lose one of its brightest lights?* he wondered. He went to Ezra and said to him, "Come learn in the yeshivah. I will support you." With thanks to the Almighty Ezra began his studies in the new yeshivah, Ohel Mo'ed. Soon he became one of the leading students, and his greatness finally became known to the public.

For forty-five years Ezra served as *rosh yeshivah* of Porat Yosef. Thousands of his students have followed in his footsteps and spread the knowledge of Torah.

RABBI ARYEH LEVIN

Rabbi Aryeh Levin was born on 6 Nissan 5645 (1885) in Orla, a small village near Bialistor in White Russia. His father, Rabbi Binyamin Beinish, had been the village teacher. Rabbi Binyamin and his wife, Etta, were very poor but exceptionally charitable. Aryeh's father had been earning a mere twenty rubles a month, less than a quarter of the amount poor lumberjacks earned. By the time Aryeh was born, however, his father was already too old to work.

Until the age of six Aryeh studied at home with a teacher who taught the children of the surrounding communities. When he was ready to begin studying *Chumash*, his father sent Aryeh to his uncle, Rabbi Binyamin's older brother Rabbi Azriel, in nearby Naravki. He studied there for almost a year. Then he returned home to Orla and continued his studies there with several teachers until the age of twelve.

During this period, he wanted to travel to Brisk to study in the yeshivah there. His father was reluctant, but they had so little money to support themselves he had to consent. In Brisk, Aryeh studied in the famous *Talmud Torah*. But for various reasons, after a couple of months he was no longer able to stay there. So Aryeh returned to Orla for Shavuos and began studying there in the *beis midrash*. He remained there for two years.

When Aryeh could not understand something, he asked the men in the *beis midrash*. Because he was so diligent, he was always among the first to arrive in the morning and among the last to leave at night. During the cold winter nights he would trudge to the *beis midrash* to study. Whether it was raining or snowing or bitterly cold, nothing kept him from his studies. And slowly, with the help of others, he was able to convince his father to let him leave once again.

A representative of a yeshivah recently established in Pahost, near Pinsk, had come to Orla several times to speak on behalf of the yeshivah. This was the place Aryeh decided to go to next.

After Pesach in 5657 (1897), he left home for Pahost. But he did not have enough money for the entire journey, so he stopped in Prozena, not far from his hometown. He was accepted into the yeshivah there on the recommendation of Rabbi Eliyahu Feinstein, head of the *beis din*, who also put him up at his home for a week.

Aryeh returned home for Rosh HaShanah, and after Sukkos he decided to go to the yeshivah in Slonim together with his friend Alter Heller. This time he easily received permission from his father. The boys went on their way, traveling in the direction of Bialystok. As they reached the Polish border, they were stopped by the police. Miraculously, though they did not have passports, they were released unharmed.

Once the boys were accepted into the yeshivah in Slonim, they had to find accommodations. They went from door to door, looking for families willing to host them for meals once a week, as was the custom at that time. They found a place to sleep in the yeshivah on two benches near the entrance. Between them they had a single blanket. Eventually each found his own place to sleep in the synagogue.

At the end of Elul, Aryeh went home. After Sukkos he decided he must go to Volozhin Yeshivah, which had opened less than a month before. When he arrived, he was impressed by the sounds of Torah learning — beautiful, powerful, strong — which emanated from the hundreds of students studying in the *beis midrash*. Aryeh was interviewed by Rabbi Rephael Shapiro. To Aryeh's immense disappointment Rabbi Shapiro would not accept the boy; he felt he was too young. Rabbi Meir Yaslovitz, a rebbe and advisor in the yeshivah, gave Aryeh a letter of recommendation for Rabbi Shlomo Galvintzitz, *rosh yeshivah* of the yeshivah in Maskil L'Eisan Synagogue in Minsk, and money for traveling expenses.

It was slightly before midnight when Aryeh arrived in Minsk. The first thing he did was head for the Maskil L'Eisan Synagogue. A few yeshivah students were still up learning. They welcomed Aryeh and found him a bench to sleep on. The next morning Aryeh was accepted in the yeshivah.

Aryeh had never been in Minsk before, so he didn't know any families who could host him. He managed to make arrangements for some of his meals, but there were times he went hungry. Soon after, he discovered he had a relative among the students named Yosef Werbin. He advised Aryeh to go to Slutzk, where Yosef had studied before coming to Maskil L'Eisan. And so, during Chol HaMo'ed Pesach, Aryeh set out for Slutzk.

Aryeh was accepted into the yeshivah in Slutzk. He threw himself into his studies and became close with the Ridbaz and

Rabbi Isser Zalman Meltzer, the *rosh yeshivah*, who had welcomed him warmly. Aryeh studied there for three years.

Years later, Rabbi Isser Zalman Meltzer found out that Aryeh had often gone hungry while he was at the yeshivah. Rabbi Meltzer was extremely upset and cried out to him, "What will I say on the Day of Judgment? Why didn't I know that you slept on a bench and did not eat?" The *rosh yeshivah* did not let Aryeh leave until he forgave him and promised that he did not hold a grudge against him.

After three years in Slutzk, Aryeh returned to Orla and began preparations to emigrate to Eretz Yisrael. But his father was very sick, and their financial situation was dire: the night before Aryeh returned home, the only cow from which the family got a little milk and butter had collapsed. Later in life, when Aryeh told this story, he would say that he never forgot the pain in his mother's eyes that night, because she had nothing but stale black bread to serve her son, whom she had not seen for several years.

Eventually, Aryeh made it to Eretz Yisrael. There he became known as the "father of prisoners," because he visited the Jewish prisoners held by the British there.

RABBI MATZLIACH MAZUZ

R abbi Matzliach Mazuz was born on a Friday evening, 26 Marcheshvan 5672 (1912), in Gorba, to Rabbi Rephael and Rachel.

Matzliach spent his early years in Ariena, approximately 140 kilometers outside Tunis. The city of his childhood was known for its clear, crisp air. In that beautiful, comfortable setting, Matzliach's father taught him Torah in his free time. Matzliach also studied with Rabbi Yehudah Chagag. When he graduated from learning *Chumash* to the Talmud class, Matzliach couldn't find a *chavrusa*. There was no one on his level who could learn with him. Even the rebbe had difficulty; Matzliach had outgrown the school in Ariena.

Rabbi Rephael would return home from a long day at his store to find his wife weeping. She would plead with him to return to Gorba, a city full of *talmidei chachamim* who could teach Matzliach and help him reach his potential. Every day she would say to herself, *I would rather live in a small, dark house in poverty so my son could study Torah.* Rabbi Rephael could not resist her pleading. He sold his store and their house for less than they were worth and returned to Gorba at the end of 5682 (1922).

The first night of their return to Gorba they stayed at the home of Rabbi Rephael's brother Menachem. Menachem showed Matzliach a notebook of original insights written by his son when he was thirteen. Matzliach read the title on the front, "Rabbi Chananiah, the Deputy of the *Kohanim*," and skimmed through the pages that followed. They were filled with crowded script written in fluent Spanish. Then came another title, "Chizkeyah and Rabbi Avahu," followed by more insights. Impressed, Matzliach asked his uncle to explain what was written in the notebook. His uncle told him they were original ideas his son had written down on various topics in the Talmud. Then he added, "Do you think you could write something like this?"

Matzliach did not answer. He was too busy thinking. *I must be able to do this, no matter what.* All the pleasures of his childhood in Ariena, all the toys and games, became unimportant. All he could think about now was becoming a *gadol b'Torah*.

At the age of twelve, Matzliach traveled with his father to Tunisia, where he would have an operation to remove his tonsils. At that time a well-known *rav*, Rabbi David Keturah, who later served as Tunisia's chief rabbi, lived there. Every Shabbos, scholars and rabbis came to him to study *Shulchan Aruch*, which he would teach by heart with the explanations of the commentaries, including *Tur* and *Beis Yosef*. Rabbi Rephael and Matzliach were among the *rav*'s visitors the Shabbos they were in Tunisia.

Rabbi Rephael asked Rabbi David if Matzliach could learn with him and show him what he was up to in his studies. Rabbi David agreed. Matzliach explained thoroughly a topic in *Pesachim* with all the commentaries, adding several insights of his own. The rabbi intently followed everything Matzliach had to say, allowing him to finish, though the men were waiting for him to begin his lecture on *Shulchan Aruch*. When Matzliach was finished, Rabbi David nicknamed him the "new Eliyahu HaNavi." From then on, Rabbi David showed him the respect one accords a *talmid chacham*.

When the family had returned to Gorba, Rabbi Rephael opened a grocery store, but it was not successful. Eventually he lost all the money he had made in Ariena. Hoping a change of location would help, Rabbi Rephael moved his store to Medanin, a suburb of Gorba, but again he did not succeed. Eventually he was penniless, and his meals consisted of the raw seeds he sold in his store. Surprisingly, he did not despair. He was content that Matzliach was progressing in his studies. When he would ask his son's rebbe, Rabbi Rachamim Chai Chavitah, how Matzliach was doing and the rabbi told him he was learning well, Rabbi Rephael felt like a millionaire.

Still, his happiness over Matzliach's learning could not feed his family, and he was forced to return to Tunis to work. He left his son and wife alone in their home in Gorba and sent them money every month so Matzliach could continue studying. Rabbi Rephael himself would make due with what was left. Within six months he returned to Gorba for the holidays.

Matzliach studied in Gorba for seven and a half years. Night after night he sat, surrounded by *sefarim*, until dawn, when he went to pray in the shul. Then, until the time came for him to go to his rebbe's class, Matzliach would sit at home and study quietly. As a child, he had always wanted a watch so he could plan his time exactly — so much time for praying, so much for eating and sleeping, and the rest for learning Gemara and halachah.

Aside from the set classes each day, the students in Gorba

studied every morning and evening to gain a broader knowledge of the Talmud. The rebbe also gave the students questions on *Shulchan Aruch*. Each student was required to bring the answers to the rebbe on Shabbos. The rebbe would then review the answer and give the student his comments. In the beginning, the rebbe provided the sources where the boys could find the answers. Later, when they became more proficient, he left out the sources, and they would have to figure out the answers entirely by themselves.

When Matzliach had children of his own, he told them about a game he loved to play as a child, in which he would "compete" with the rabbi of Tunis, Rabbi Yitzchak Tiv, who had written *Erech HaShulchan*. He would study all the halachos on a given subject without looking at the *Erech HaShulchan*. When he had learned through the topic thoroughly, he would open the *sefer* and see what it said on the subject he had just studied. If the *Erech HaShulchan* cited a source Matzliach had not found, he would take careful note of it and learn it the next time. This is how he studied halachah.

Matzliach reviewed everything he learned several times. He would say to his friends, "Ask me a difficult question in halachah, and I will answer it." He also kept a record of the more difficult halachic questions asked by the commentators.

In 5686 (1926), when Matzliach was fourteen years old, he was invited to the wedding of his cousin Ben Tzion. He was required to attend, though it would take time from his studies and he was in the middle of several difficult Talmudic topics. He sat among the guests and studied the Gemara by heart, with commentaries. From time to time he would leave the wedding party and go into a side room, where he'd jot down a note to himself to remember what he had studied. Then he'd return to his place at the wedding.

By the time Matzliach was sixteen, he had already written responsa of great length. Among these responsa was an answer on the subject of whether you are permitted to study Arabic and math in the synagogue. He dealt with this question by discussing in great detail the Talmud and codifiers and came to the conclusion that it is permissible. His responsa was sent to the *gaon* Rabbi Ovadiah Hadayah in Jerusalem, and it was later published in the *rav*'s *sefer Yaskil L'David*. When Rabbi Ovadiah first saw the responsa, he thought a great *talmid chacham* had written it. He wrote a letter requesting that the author help Rabbi Ovadiah raise money for Beis El, a Kabbalah yeshivah where Rabbi Ovadiah taught. Matzliach, of course, had to decline; he himself was still a student in yeshivah and was not familiar with how to raise money.

Once the rebbe asked Matzliach a question on the mitzvah of fulfilling the wishes of a deceased. Three weeks passed, and Matzliach had not presented an answer to his rebbe. His rebbe said to him, "What is taking you so long? You can't have written more than a few pages on the subject." Matzliach showed his rebbe the three hundred pages he had already written, and he was still not finished.

His rebbe used to tell how he would give Matzliach and the other students questions on various topics — Pesach, kashrus, marriage, inheritance — so the boys would gain an extensive knowledge of halachah. Over the seven-and-a-half-year period that Matzliach learned in Gorba he advanced to higher and higher levels. When he was sixteen, he was ready to begin studying Kabbalah.

When Matzliach was eighteen he got married. The time for the wedding to start arrived, and the guests were coming, but the groom was nowhere to be found. They asked his rebbe, who told them that Matzliach was probably in the synagogue library, where he liked to study. They headed for the library and did indeed find Matzliach sitting there, learning. "I already showered and dressed. When they call for me I will come, but it is a pity to waste time waiting."

This was his way. Matzliach would not waste even a moment.

Matzliach became a *dayan* in the Tunis *beis din* and the author of *Ish Matzliach*.

RABBI REPHAEL BARUCH TOLEDANO

Rabbi Rephael Baruch Toledano was born in 5650 (1890) in Méknes, Morocco. His father, Rabbi Yaakov, was the chief rabbi, and his mother was a righteous woman named Chanah.

Rephael loved to learn Torah from when he was child. Every year he advanced further in his studies and started learning Kabbalah at a young age.

When he was ten years old, Rephael became very ill. The name *Rephael*, which means "Hashem heals," was added to his given name, *Baruch*. His parents hoped the new name would be a good omen for him and he would get better. Rephael's childhood friend, Yosef Mashash, who would one day serve as chief rabbi of Haifa, came to visit him. Rephael was writhing and moaning in pain. Suddenly, his father entered the room. Rephael immediately stopped groaning, tightly pursing his lips, so his father would not realize how great his pain really was. When Yosef asked him why he had stopped crying, Rephael answered, "I didn't want to upset my father."

Eventually Rephael recovered, and he was able to continue on his path to greatness. Rephael became close with the great Torah scholars in Méknes and learned Torah from them. The spiritual teacher who molded his personality was the *dayan* of Méknes, Rabbi Chaim Mashash. His primary rebbe was the extraordinary *gaon* Rabbi Chaim Birdogo, the *rosh yeshivah*. He showed Rephael the depths of Torah, and in a few short years under his tutelage Rephael developed into a recognized expert in the Talmud and halachah.

When Rephael studied, he researched a topic until he discovered its true meaning. He avoided sophistry and far-fetched explanations. This search for the truth was what guided his every effort.

When he attained extensive knowledge of the Talmud and halachah, Rephael began studying Kabbalah with Rabbi Yosef Alkobi, a renowned Kabbalist. Rephael excelled in his study of Kabbalah and became an expert in the *Zohar*, *Sefer Tekunim*, and the writings of the Ari. Rephael became known as one of the greatest *talmidei chachamim* in the country.

RABBI MORDECHAI AMAYIS HAKOHEN

Rabbi Mordechai Amayis HaKohen was born around the year 5646 (1886). His father was Yitzchak HaKohen, known for his piety and honesty. Reb Yitzchak spent much of his time learning Torah, working on behalf of the community, and doing *chesed*. His wife, Aziza, was a charitable and kind woman.

As a child, Mordechai studied under Rabbi Yosef Barabi. Mordechai was not like many other *gedolim*, who had unusual intellectual abilities from the beginning. Mordechai could be described by the verse "Your beginning was with pain, and in the end you became great forever" (Iyov 8:7). It was only as a result of hard work and immense effort that he merited distinguished positions and acquired greatness in Torah.

When Mordechai was sixteen, he married his niece. After his marriage, his father wanted him to leave the *beis midrash* and learn a trade. Mordechai stubbornly refused. He continued studying for another year but was still considered an unexceptional student. His father, a goldsmith, did not hold out any longer. He insisted that Mordechai stop learning and become his apprentice. Mordechai did not want to leave. He broke out in tears and expressed his love for learning. His father told him it was normal for a person to study Torah, then learn a trade. Mordechai had completed his years of study, and according to his rebbe, he would never be able to become a rabbi. There was no sense in him continuing his studies in the *beis midrash*.

Mordechai listened in silence to what his father was telling him, but all the time he was thinking, *Is there anything Hashem cannot do?* He decided he would devote his heart and soul to learning Torah until his father would see that he was worthy of the crown of Torah.

Hashem helped Mordechai in the form of the chief rabbi of Gorba, Rabbi Moshe Zakan Mazuz. When the *rav* heard about the disagreement between Mordechai and his father, Rabbi Mazuz sent a sarcastic letter to Mordechai's father: "I heard your son Mordechai does not want to help you support the family and only wants to study Torah. This cannot be. How can you bear the burden of supporting your son's family while he learns? Will the Torah bring in money?" Rabbi Yitzchak got the point. He admitted his mistake and allowed Mordechai to remain in the *beis midrash*.

Mordechai did not disappoint his father. Soon it was obvious that there was a big difference between Mordechai the boy and Mordechai the man. He began to surpass the other students in his class, and within ten years Mordechai was selected to serve as a *dayan* in Gorba alongside his rebbe. Eventually he took over the position of chief rabbi of Gorba and then chief rabbi of all of Tunisia, and he wrote the *sefer Gedulas Mordechai*.

RABBI SHLOMO MUTZFI

A t midnight one Friday evening during the month of Shevat 5660 (1900) the house of the *tzaddik* Rabbi Tzion Meir Mutzfi was full of hustle and bustle. The *rebbetzin* was giving birth. Soon the house was illuminated by a bright light; it was the light of dawn, the moment when their firstborn son was born. Joy and happiness reigned, for the great Kabbalah scholar Rabbi Shlomo Mutzfi had been brought into the world.

Shlomo's parents gave him a classic Torah education. When he was two years old, his father started taking him to shul. The child saw the *gedolim* of the time praying and studying, and he learned from them. At the age of five, Shlomo began attending elementary school. By the time he was six he had learned how to read Torah with the right melody, just like a chazzan. One Shabbos, the reader made a mistake during the reading of the Torah which the congregation did not catch. Young Shlomo yelled out the correction to the chazzan. His grandfather, a modest man, hid Shlomo under his tallis so the congregation wouldn't know who was the amazing young child who knew how to read the Torah so perfectly.

Shlomo's deeds were not known, but his modesty and humility were. One typical incident happened when he was only six. Guests from abroad were scheduled to visit and observe at Shlomo's school, together with the leaders of the community and the chief rabbi of Baghdad. As the best student of his class, Shlomo was chosen by the principal to be presented before the guests. The principal hoped they would be impressed by his advanced level and it would enhance the school's reputation.

But young Shlomo had something else in mind. He told the principal firmly that he was not willing to appear before the guests, because he did not want to be singled out as a better student and cause bad feelings between himself and his friends. When the principal insisted that he appear before the guests, Shlomo told the principal he would run away. The principal posted a guard at the entrance to the school, so Shlomo would not be able to leave the building.

When the guests arrived, Shomo tried to run away; but the doors were locked and a guard was sitting by the entrance. He was trapped. Later in life he described what he went through at that moment. "For over two hours I suffered terrible pains, because I did not want to do anything that would cause me to be arrogant."

Shlomo was nine years old when Rabbi Yosef Chaim, the Ben Ish Chai, passed away. Shlomo attended the funeral and mourned over the death of this great *tzaddik*. At the funeral, Shlomo promised to himself that he would study Torah with greater diligence and act piously to help fill the void left by the passing of this great leader.

From that day, Shlomo was like an overflowing spring and filled with a new spirit. He became more devout and set himself apart from the world more and more. His entire focus was on studying Torah.

Shlomo's parents tried to get him to moderate his behavior. But Shlomo continued in his own way. He decided to wake up every night at midnight and study Torah until dawn, as his father did. To do this, first he had to figure out a way to wake up at midnight. He thought about it for a while and came up with an idea. He tied a rope around his hand and attached the other end to the door latch. When his father would get up at midnight and open the front door, the rope would pull on Shlomo's hand and he, too, would wake up.

For two weeks this idea worked, until one night his father noticed the rope tied to the door latch and took it off. But nothing can stand in the way of a person's resolve, and Shlomo found another way to wake up. He tied a rope to his hand and let the other end of the rope hang down outside his window in the back of the house. He asked a friend whose parents let him get up at midnight to pull on the rope when he passed by Shlomo's house. Each night, after his father left, Shlomo's friend would come by and wake Shlomo up. Together they would go to the *beis midrash*, hide in a corner, and study until dawn. During this time, they studied both Talmud and *mussar*. They would memorize what they learned so they could put it into practice.

Shlomo's mother once told the following story: "When my son was twelve years old, he would stand in the courtyard of the house every Friday night and recite all of Tehillim. The wall next to him would begin to shake and crumble. I would plead with him to come into the house and say *tehillim* inside, but he refused, not wanting to disturb his little brothers, who were sleeping."

Shlomo valued each moment as if it were an expensive jewel. He would carefully think through every action. He conducted himself like the *gedolim* of the generation — holy and separate, pious and industrious. These were the extraordinary traits of Shlomo Mutzfi, the young *tzaddik*.

RABBI CHAIM SANUNE

On the ninth day of Tishrei, a few hours before Yom Kippur began, the young Rebbetzin Yiman felt the first pangs of childbirth. She was the wife of the pious Kabbalah scholar Rabbi Yichyeh Sanune of the Bida family. By nightfall the *rebbetzin* had given birth to a boy. The birth of this child brought great joy to the village of San'a, for Rabbi Yichyeh, a teacher of young children, was beloved and respected by all who knew him.

For the first seven days after the baby was born, villagers came to the house of Rabbi Yichyeh and studied Torah there as a protection for the newborn and and as a *segulah* for his future spiritual and material success. When the eve of his bris came, which fell out during Chol HaMo'ed Sukkos, the house filled with guests, among them Rabbi Shlomo Ben Aharon, who served as head of the *beis din* there. As was the custom, they all studied selections from the *Zohar* and other *sefarim*. Before sunrise they prayed *shacharis* and then made the bris, welcoming the newborn, who was named Chaim, into the covenant of our forefather Avraham.

Like many great rabbis, Chaim merited from an early age to hear words of Torah. When he was an infant, his mother insisted on placing his carriage next to the wall of their house, which adjoined a synagogue, so he would hear words of Torah. Her efforts bore fruit — Chaim later merited to become a great Torah scholar.

As a boy, Chaim went to study in the yeshivah where his father taught. There he learned to read and went on to study *Chumash*, Mishnah, Talmud, and halachah.

In those days, it was difficult to study in a yeshivah in Yemen because there were no publishers, which resulted in a shortage of printed books. *Sefarim* that came in from the west were snatched up in the market. The situation was so bad that twenty children would have to share a single *sefer*. The children adapted, and with time they learned to read from any side — even upside down.

The lack of books was not an obstacle for young Chaim. He grew in Torah, helped by a phenomenal memory. But Chaim did not rely only on his extraordinary intellect. Diligently he studied, day and night, following in the footsteps of the Yemenite scholars who would begin their day at midnight.

These scholars would start with *Tikun Chatzos* (prayers recited at midnight in memory of the destruction of the Beis HaMikdash), which they recited with great emotion. Tears ran down their cheeks from the anguish they felt over the exile of the Jewish people. After reciting *Tikun Chatzos*, they would study Gemara until it was time to pray *shacharis*, after which they studied halachah, Mishnah, and Gemara in depth. This continued until an hour or so after the evening prayers.

Chaim kept this rigorous schedule, and he was very young

when he received rabbinical ordination from his father. His reputation as a scholar spread throughout the village, but he was not interested in fame. His only desire was to listen and learn. And so, after receiving permission from his parents, he left the village in which he grew up for the great Torah centers of his homeland, where the sounds of Torah learning could be heard day and night.

At that time, the best and most devoted students learned under the rabbi and Kabbalist Rabbi Shlomo ben Yosef Tabib and Rabbi David Yashish Chadad. Before they could enter the yeshivah, the boys were thoroughly tested by Rabbi Shlomo and Rabbi David. Only those who passed the difficult test were admitted, and only a few outstanding students merited to study with these great scholars.

Chaim succeeded in gaining admission to the yeshivah. He studied Torah as never before, and soon he was at the top of his class. His greatest aspiration was to be in the company of the two great rabbis who ran the yeshivah. Chaim not only absorbed their Torah knowledge, but he also learned *mussar* and *derech eretz* from them. To him their ways were a perfect, living example of a Torah-true lifestyle. He became so attached to his teachers that they knew all his thoughts and desires. Recognizing his fine personality and rare intellect, they in turn encouraged Chaim to ascend higher on the spiritual ladder.

Chaim did not let himself rest. Day and night he sat, concentrating on his Gemara, not wasting a single moment. He studied the words of our Sages with great intensity and devotion and observed their teachings in all aspects of his daily life.

RABBI YAAKOV MUTZFI

Rabbi Yaakov Mutzfi, rabbi of the Eidah Chareidis (the religious community) of Jerusalem, was born in 5660 (1900) in Baghdad. In his youth, he studied Torah in the Beis Zilkah Yeshivah. There, with his extraordinary intellect, he stood out like a bright diamond. To be so distinguished he had to be truly exceptional — at Beis Zilkah hundreds of young Jewish boys gathered, among them those who became the scholars and rabbis of the Sephardic Jews, to study Torah.

What young Yaakov was especially noted for was his diligence and intensity. At the age of seven, he had trained himself to wake up at midnight to study Talmud and *mussar* deep into the night. Then he would make his way to shul, stopping first at the home of a friend, whom he'd wake up by pulling on a rope that was hanging out of the window — the other end of the rope was tied to his friend's arm. This other boy was Shlomo Mutzfi, about whom the book *The World of the Tzaddik* was later written.

The boys would walk to the synagogue and study together in

a corner where they could be inconspicuous. For the first two hours, they'd learn *mussar*; the rest of the night was spent on Gemara, until it was time to pray. Later in life Rabbi Shlomo Mutzfi recalled, "I used to be very diligent. I needed only two hours of sleep a night, and I'd study for eighteen hours without stopping to eat or rest. My friend Yaakov Mutzfi and I would hide in a corner of the *beis midrash* so know one would see us. Often our parents sent someone to fetch us back home so we'd eat something or get some sleep, but they could never find us."

When Rabbi Yaakov was older, he'd talk about the importance of learning Torah even in difficult situations. He would say, "A person cannot measure the reward for studying Torah." Once he spoke about the days when he studied Talmud and halachah with the *gaon* Rabbi Solmon Chugi Abudi in a *kollel* in Beis Zilkah eighteen hours a day. Those in the *kollel* received such a small sum of money that it was enough for Yaakov to buy only a little bread and something to drink. He would go to the *beis midrash* on Sunday mornings and stay there all week, returning home only on Fridays for Shabbos.

At that time the students in Beis Zilkah heard that a new yeshivah had opened, where there were more wealthy supporters. Those in the *kollel* were receiving almost twenty times the amount Yaakov was getting in Beis Zilkah. Many switched to this other yeshivah because of the difficult conditions they endured in Beis Zilkah. But Yaakov and his friend Shlomo weren't in such a hurry to leave — they had heard that the new yeshivah was not as outstanding as Beis Zilkah. Though the situation was difficult, they remained in Beis Zilkah to uphold the quality of their Torah.

RABBI MORDECHAI SHARABI

Rabbi Mordechai Sharabi's grandfather was Rabbi Yefes Avraham Taazi, who served for many years as head of the Sharab *beis din*. Rabbi Yefes Avraham was known for his saintliness, and he was one of the outstanding Torah scholars of his time. With his long beard he had the appearance of an angel. Rabbi Yefes Avraham's son Rabbi Yehudah married the saintly Miriam. Rabbi Yehudah died at a young age, leaving behind a daughter and a pregnant wife.

In 5672 (1912) Rabbi Mordechai Sharabi was born. His birth brought great joy to the family. Sadly, when he was not quite two years old, his mother passed away, unable to withstand the pressures and trials of a widow's life.

Mordechai first went to school in the community yeshivah. Since he was very bright, his grandfather set aside several hours a day to teach him. Rabbi Yefes Avraham was concerned about *ayin hara*, "the evil eye," which could incur strict judgment from Heaven and cause bad things to happen; he pinned on his grandson a silver pin with the names of holy persons to protect him. Mordechai wore this pin for most of his life, until 5738 (1977), when he gave it to one of his students.

Mordechai was appointed as a teacher of more than a hundred sixteen- and seventeen-year-old students when he was only eight years old. Despite the age difference, Mordechai was far more advanced than his students. During his class there was complete silence, as his students sat close together listening intently to Mordechai's every word. They loved his *shiur*, because his manner of teaching was very pleasant and easygoing. Mordechai taught in this way so his lesson would be understood by all.

Mordechai also taught tractate *Shabbos* to young children in another town. He did not simply explain the *gemara* he was teaching; he also taught them the halachos of Shabbos. His grandfather had a loom for weaving in his house. Mordechai brought it to school to explain the complicated laws of weaving on Shabbos.

Mordechai became a disciple of the Kabbalist Rabbi Chaim Sanune, head of the San'a *beis din*. The story of how Mordechai came to Rabbi Chaim is an interesting one.

Rabbi Chaim first met Mordechai when he was nine years old. Mordechai, an orphan, was traveling with a saintly old man, wandering from town to town to bring Torah to those living in remote villages. Mordechai held a rod in one hand to prod the animal they rode. In the other was a *sefer* from which he studied Torah. Rabbi Chaim was passing by when he saw this. He asked the old sage, "What is this boy like? What is he to you?"

The old man answered, "This is Mordechai the son of Rabbi Yehudah, who passed away. I took him into my house to bring him up in a Torah environment."

Rabbi Chaim, impressed by the boy's extraordinary behavior, asked the elderly sage to leave Mordechai with him so they could study Torah and halachah together. The old man could not refuse in the face of Rabbi Chaim's persistence and left Mordechai with the great rabbi. Mordechai stayed with Rabbi Chaim for two years.

Word of Mordechai's greatness reached the chief rabbi of the Sharab *beis din*, Rabbi Salim Said. He liked Mordechai so much that he took him to his city, Elchada, which was a great Jewish center at the time and where the *beis din* for Yemenite Jews convened. Though still very young when he went to live with Rabbi Salim, the scholars of Elchada quickly came to recognize Mordechai's greatness. Soon he was known as a *gaon* and a holy person.

Mordechai assisted the chief rabbi by answering questions sent to him from all over Yemen. Mordechai's responses were exceptionally clear and sharp.

At his bar mitzvah celebration, Mordechai mesmerized his listeners with his discourse on a very difficult explanation of the laws of kashrus. Shortly thereafter, Mordechai left the home of the chief rabbi — the leaders of another city, Gabel Chabshi, had asked the chief rabbi to send them a teacher of Torah. Rabbi Salim Said could not think of a better person to teach Jewish children than Mordechai — though he was only fourteen at the time.

THE BABA SALI

On Rosh HaShanah 5650 (1890) the great *tzaddik*, Kabbalist, and miracle worker known as the Baba Sali was born. The whole town filled the Abuchatzeira home to celebrate Yisrael's bris.

Yisrael's father, Rabbi Masoud Abuchatzeira, and his wife raised her son with great devotion. She did not allow maids to help in their home so she alone could be involved in raising the boy. She believed that from the time a child is born, while he is still in the cradle, one must be careful that he not see or hear improper things, and that even a baby who cannot speak or understand should hear words of Torah. Thus the house in which Yisrael grew up was filled with Torah and *chesed*.

Yisrael learned alef-beis at home with a private teacher. He quickly learned how to read and began learning *Chumash* at a very young age. He loved learning *Chumash* and preferred that to going out to play with the other children.

With natural curiosity, young Yisrael watched carefully when his father and older brother Rabbi David sat down to eat. But it was difficult to find them eating during the week. Later it was explained to him that they fasted often, and that when they did eat during the week they ate very little — just enough to provide basic sustenance. He immediately understood that there is a strong connection between a person's growth in Torah and faith in the Almighty and abstinence from eating and other pleasures.

What made an indelible impression on Yisrael was the manner in which his father and brother walked on the street. The few times he observed his father walking outside, he learned that one should lower the scarf that covers one's head over the eyes so as to avoid seeing a forbidden sight.

Yisrael began to immerse in a mikveh at a very young age, when he began to understand that serving God in holiness is very important. He also took upon himself another practice which children of his age normally did not do: he fasted. At first he took upon himself short fasts, and his parents did not realize what he was doing.

When Yisrael turned twelve, during the Shovevim (the eight weeks in a leap year when we read the first eight *parashiyos* of *sefer Shemos*), which is a time that is particularly appropriate for *teshuvah*, he decided to fast a *ta'anis hafsakah* — a fast that begins at the end of one Shabbos and concludes at the beginning of the following Shabbos. He succeeded in fasting until Friday without anyone realizing it. Feeling very weak from the week of fasting, he made his way to the mikveh on Friday. There he met his older brother Rabbi David, who, when he saw how frail and weak Yisrael was, understood that his younger brother was finishing a long fast. Rabbi David became angry and told Yisrael that he was much too young to be fasting for so long. But Yisrael felt differently. He was charting his own special course for spiritual development.

At his bar mitzvah celebration, Yisrael's extraordinary personality became evident to the community — the speech he gave was so exceptional that it was the talk of the town. From that day forward everyone in the community treated Yisrael with respect and began asking him for his blessing.

At that time, Yisrael was admitted to the local yeshivah. This was a momentous occasion, because he was much younger than the other students. Despite his age, he followed the schedule of the older students in the yeshivah. At midnight they awoke to recite *Tikun Chatzos*. Then they studied Kabbalah until just before sunrise. Before *shacharis* they went to the mikveh and then prayed with the sunrise. Then they studied *Chok L'Yisrael* in depth. After breakfast they studied Gemara until *minchah*. After praying *minchah* and *ma'ariv*, they studied *Shulchan Aruch* until they could no longer keep their eyes open. They slept until midnight, when they began their day anew.

After studying like this for several years, Yisrael became a great scholar. He was an expert in many tractates of the Talmud and its early commentaries. He also gained a complete knowledge of other Torah subjects, as well as the laws of *shechitah*, bris milah, and *safrus*. He studied whatever was necessary to become a complete Torah scholar. He also spent time alone fasting, sometimes for short periods of time and sometimes longer, analyzing his personal progress.

When he was sixteen years old, Yisrael married Pirchah. Their wedding was a day of celebration for the entire community. After he married, he decided to conduct himself with even more saintliness. His wife assisted him so he could serve his Creator in the manner he had chosen for himself. She saw her husband only on Shabbos. For her self-sacrifice and devotion she merited to be the wife of a great *tzaddik*.

THE STEIPLER GAON

Rabbi Yaakov Yisrael Kanievsky, author of *Kehilas Yaakov*, was born on 9 Tamuz 5659 (1899). His father, Rabbi Chaim Peretz, who devoted his time to Torah study, spent a great deal of time and effort raising his firstborn son. He studied *mussar* with him and taught him principles of faith. Each day he would wake him up early in the morning and teach him from *Bas Ayin*. On Shabbos he would learn with Yaakov Yisrael the *sefer Shoshanas HaAmakim*.

In his free time, Yaakov Yisrael studied from the *mussar sefarim* he found in his house and read biographies of great Torah scholars. His mother, Bracha, encouraged him to go to listen to the traveling *maggidim* who passed through the town from time to time to inspire and strengthen the people's faith. She was a great help to her husband in educating their children and was active in the community to keep Torah strong in the town.

In those days, there were no educational institutions for very young children — there were no *cheders* and no schools. The parents were responsible for teaching their children. Rabbi Chaim

Peretz and his wife, Bracha, prayed hard that their efforts would bear fruit and that their children would grow in Torah and perform mitzvos.

Young Yaakov Yisrael, healthy and robust, put all his energy into learning Torah. Together with his two brothers, a cousin, and a boy from another town, he learned Gemara with his father, Rabbi Chaim Peretz. After several hours of study, Rabbi Chaim would close his Gemara and send the boys off to rest and play for a half-hour. All the children would run out and play — all of them, that is, but Yaakov Yisrael, who would lean against the back wall of the house and continue to study.

In the evening hours, Bracha would hurry the boy off to sleep. Yaakov Yisrael would leave his Torah world for a few moments and take a book of stories about the great rabbis of old. Then he would eat something and go to bed. The young boy, tired from his busy day, would fall asleep right away.

Yaakov Yisrael became more and more immersed in the world of Torah. Gradually, his goals became more focused — focused on a life of Torah. He decided to stop reading stories about Torah scholars, instead devoting that time to halachah or Mishnah. He reached his decision that Torah would be his life before he turned twelve, and with great determination applied himself even more to learning Torah.

Soon after, Rabbi Chaim Peretz sent his son to study in a yeshivah in the village of Krimzuk, which had been established by former students of Slobodka Yeshivah. Sixty students attended this new school, ages fourteen through eighteen. Young rebbes taught these students Torah and *mussar*. When Yaakov Yisrael first arrived at the yeshivah, he studied without interruption and advanced quickly. At night he slept on a wooden bench. Every morning, eager to start his day, he awoke early and learned a chapter of *mussar*. Then he davened *shacharis* and learned Gemara the rest of the day.

One of the richest Jews in Russia, Mr. Gur Aryeh, lived in the town. He supported the yeshivah singlehandedly. On Shabbos he invited the best students to his home for the meals. Yaakov Yisrael was a regular guest in the Aryeh home. The other boys were always eager to hear about the meals he ate at the wealthy man's home. Yaakov Yisrael would tell them that he had nothing to say — they should ask the other boys who had been there.

Yaakov Yisrael studied in the yeshivah for a full year, until Rosh Chodesh Nissan 5670 (1910). Then came terrible news. The *rosh yeshivah* went to see Yaakov Yisrael to inform him that he was to return home immediately.

"Get up, my student," he said to the boy. "Get up from your studies. You must travel home. Other mitzvos are now incumbent upon you."

Yaakov Yisrael was just eleven years old at the time. Apprehensively he held the hands of his *rosh yeshivah* and tried to read his eyes. "Why must I return home? Why so suddenly? What about my studies?"

The *rosh yeshivah* sent the young boy home along with another student. On the way, the boy informed Yaakov Yisrael that his father had died. Yaakov Yisrael cried when he heard the news, and the other boy comforted him as they headed toward Yaakov Yisrael's home.

During that time the *Alter* of Slobodka established his great yeshivah in Novardok. He had great plans to establish a network of yeshivos, large and small, throughout Russia to save young Jews from the influence of the *Haskalah* movement. He sent his students out into the world spread the word of Torah among the people. These faithful students went to numerous cities and villages and established yeshivos and schools for the public.

These messengers of goodwill came even to the little Ukrainian village of Teshen. They approached Yaakov Yisrael's mother and asked her to allow her son to go with them. She agreed happily. With her difficult financial situation in mind she commented, "At least my son will have what to eat." The young boy went with them to their central location in one of the synagogues in a nearby village. From there the group traveled to the main yeshivah in Navordok. Yaakov Yisrael was eleven and a half years old when he arrived at that illustrious yeshivah.

On the ninth day of Tamuz 5672 (1912) Yaakov Yisrael reached the age of thirteen. There was no one to prepare a large meal in honor of the occasion, and his beloved mother wanted to come and bless him, but she was unable to. He received for his bar mitzvah a bowl of soup, and with this he celebrated his bar mitzvah. He had to give a speech, but he had no one to teach him because he was an orphan. He solved this problem by studying a Talmudic discourse by himself on the subject of whether one wears tefillin on Shabbos.

On the day of his bar mitzvah, Yaakov Yisrael decided that he would conduct the rest of his life in a particular way, but he did not disclose this to anyone. In his youth, he was unsure as to how he should best serve God given his personality and needs, so he decided that his goals would be "to know the entire Talmud, Babylonian and Jerusalem; to study diligently; to pray sincerely; and to be careful in the performance of the mitzvos." He also decided that in addition to studying the Talmudic tractate that was being studied in the yeshivah he would study an additional tractate from the section of *Mo'ed*. Thus he learned *Beitzah*, then *Sukkah*, and finally *Shabbos* and *Eiruvin*. After that he devoted time to studying the section of *Kodshim*. Later in life he said that by the age of fifteen he had already compiled a notebook of original Torah insights on *Nedarim*.

In 5676 (1916), when Yaakov Yisrael was seventeen, he was sent by the *Alter* of Novardok to set up and lead a yeshivah in the city of Rogotchov. During Chol HaMo'ed Pesach, news came that the Russian army had come to the city to search for deserters. On the seventh night of Pesach, the army burst into the yeshivah and forcibly took Yaakov Yisrael. After some pleading they allowed him to take with him his tefillin, a Gemara, and a copy of *Chayei Adam*. He wrote the first section of his monumental work *Kehilas Yaakov* while he was in the army.

When he was brought to the army camp, he was given a uniform and ordered to put it on. Yaakov Yisrael was concerned that the uniform might have *sha'atnez*, so he asked the officer in charge if they could give him other clothes that he could be sure did not have any *sha'atnez*. The officer did not understand his request. Yaakov Yisrael had to write a letter in Russian explaining to his superiors that the uniform was not in keeping with his religious requirements. His superiors passed his letter up the line to their superiors until it reached the czar himself. The czar ordered his underlings to allow Jewish soldiers to choose clothes as they saw fit. Though it was bitterly cold in the camp, Yaakov Yisrael went to a warehouse and chose summer clothes, because he was certain they did not have any *sha'atnez*.

Legendary stories are told about Yaakov Yisrael and the time he served in the Russian army with his Talmud and *Chayei Adam*. He went through some difficult experiences, yet he made sure to study Torah each day and night. The *gaon* Rabbi Ben Tzion Brok would send him, from time to time, different tractates of the Talmud in small print. He ended up sending Yaakov Yisrael half of the entire Talmud. Every free moment he had, Yaakov Yisrael could be found studying Torah with great intensity and dedication.

RABBI MOSHE FEINSTEIN

Rabbi David Feinstein and his wife did not have any children. They went to the Rebbe of Karlin-Stolin, Rabbi Yisrael, hoping that with his blessing they would be able to have children. Soon after, they did indeed have a child, and they were full of joy. Their happiness was magnified when they realized that their son, Moshe, possessed rare qualities — a fine mind and an exceptional character.

When he was six years old, Moshe and a friend had a "serious" discussion. "When I get older," his friend said to Moshe, "I want to be a tailor like my father. It is a good thing for a son to follow in in his father's footsteps."

Moshe responded, "I hope that I will be a rabbi."

Moshe was an excellent chess player in a country where chess was a popular game among Torah scholars. But when he turned eighteen, he stopped playing. Later in life he explained why: "I said to myself, *If a person is already using his brains, better that he use them to study Torah.*"

In his youth, his father, Rabbi David, was Moshe's primary

teacher. By the time he was ten, Moshe knew all of *Bava Kama*, *Bava Metzia*, and *Bava Basra* — among the most difficult four hundred pages in the Talmud. On the eve of Yom Kippur, before his bar mitzvah, he and his father stayed up all night and learned the entire tractate of *Yoma*.

As an adult, Moshe would say how his father not only taught him Torah but also taught him to be concerned with details. Rabbi David hired a private teacher for Moshe and three other boys to better develop their full intellectual abilities. This group succeeded in completing the tractate of *Gittin* with all the *Tosafos* within a year.

Shortly after Moshe's bar mitzvah his father decided that he should leave home to study under the guidance of one of the outstanding Torah giants of the time, Rabbi Isser Zalman Meltzer, *rosh yeshivah* of Eitz Chaim in Slutzk. At the yeshivah, Moshe became known as an extraordinary scholar and a very diligent student. He was called "the prodigy from Starovin." He spent many hours in the *beis midrash*, sleeping no more than five hours a night. By the time he was a teenager, Moshe knew two entire sections of the Talmud. Forty years later, Rabbi Isser Zalman Meltzer would discuss with great respect several of the questions and insights Moshe Feinstein had when he was just a teenager.

After Rabbi Moshe had became famous as one of the greatest Torah scholars of his day, a boy of fifteen asked him, "Does the *rosh yeshivah* study only those tractates in the Jerusalem Talmud which do not have a counterpart in the Babylonian Talmud or does he also study the other tractates?"

Rabbi Moshe responded with a warm smile. "Of course. When I was your age, I had already written original insights on the Jerusalem Talmud's version of *Bava Kama*, *Bava Metzia*, and *Bava Basra*." In this way Rabbi Moshe encouraged his students to realize that they, too, could accomplish great things in Torah study.

RABBI YISSACHAR DOV GOLDSTEIN

R abbi Yissachar Dov Goldstein was the author of *Ohel Yissachar*, the *rav* of the Chasam Sofer community, and the *rosh yeshivah* of Shomrei HaChomos in Jerusalem. He was born in 5675 (1915) in Pressburg, the city famous for its Torah scholars, most notably the Chasam Sofer. The sound of hundreds of boys studying Torah could be heard throughout the city and its environs day and night.

Rabbi Yissachar Dov's father, Rabbi Menachem Aharon, was a God-fearing man who was very active in charitable activities and served as the *gabbai tzedakah* for the organization Marpeh L'Nefesh. His house served as a meeting place for great Torah scholars and leaders.

As a young boy, Yissachar Dov studied in the Yesodei HaTorah Yeshivah. His diligence in learning resembled that of a much older student. It was so exceptional that he was given the nickname *Rosh Yeshivah*.

Yissachar Dov's father urged him to get some sleep, but the boy left a small light burning so he could continue studying without his father realizing it. Whenever he traveled with his family, he took along with him several *sefarim* so he would not waste even a moment.

Yissachar Dov studied with the greatest rabbis of his time, not the least of which was the *gaon* Rabbi Yosef Tzvi Dushinsky, whom Yissachar Dov regarded as his primary rebbe. Rabbi Yosef Tzvi said that he never had such a dedicated student as Yissachar Dov. When Rabbi Yosef Tzvi passed away, Yissachar Dov clung to the *gaon* from Tishban and Rabbi Zelig Reuven Bangis. He was also fortunate to become very close to the Chazon Ish.

Because of his intense dedication to learning, Yissachar Dov developed the ability to find the truth, with a clear and broad outlook. As he studied, he delved into issues with a depth beyond the capabilities of the average person. He said of himself that during his youth he studied Gemara with *Rashi* for at least ten hours a day. He also had an extraordinary memory and was able to review what he learned without looking inside the text.

The last thirty-three years of his life were dedicated to writing his monumental collection of insights on the responsa of the Chasam Sofer. This work will illuminate the Jewish world for generations to come in all aspects of Torah scholarship. His pointed comments, his precise method of analysis, his ability to support or decide questions raised by commentators who either agreed or disagreed with the Chasam Sofer, were all beyond the abilities of an average person and set his work above all others in our generation.

RABBI YOSEF ADAS

Rabbi Yosef Adas, *rosh yeshivah* of Porat Yosef, was born on 20 Tishrei 5684 (1924). His father, Rabbi Yaakov Adas, grandson of the Kabbalist Rabbi Avraham Chaim Adas, was himself *rosh yeshivah* of Porat Yosef, as well as a member of the Jerusalem *beis din*.

From a very young age, Rabbi Yosef Adas was careful to adhere to every stringency and wanted to lead a life based on Torah. When he became engaged, he said that the most important thing was that his bride agree that he would study Torah all his life.

For close to forty years Rabbi Yosef taught in Porat Yosef, in addition to a class for adult men in the Beis Yisrael neighborhood of Jerusalem. For twenty-five years he taught a morning class at the Western Wall. He taught his classes with an eye on the clock, careful to begin and end exactly at the scheduled times. Rabbi Yosef's attention to such details are a lesson in ethics and a prime example of how a pious person serves his Creator.

Rabbi Yosef started his day at two-thirty in the morning to

say *Tikun Chatzos*. Then he immersed in the mikveh and studied until sunrise, when he prayed *shacharis*. He prayed at sunrise every day throughout his life. And, except on Shabbos and *yom tov*, he prayed at the Western Wall.

When he finished praying *shacharis*, he would take a short nap and eat a small meal. Then he was off to Porat Yosef to teach his classes, which began at nine. In the afternoon he gave an intensive lecture for businessmen in the Shaul Tzedakah synagogue. Careful never to miss a lecture, he completed most of *Shas* with these men. Even when he had a family celebration to attend, he would leave the celebration and give his class, then return later to the family event. Never would he cancel or ask someone to take over for him.

After the lecture, he would walk to the Ohel Rachel synagogue on the outskirts of the Bucharin neighborhood and study Kabbalah. At eleven he returned home and dealt with community matters, helping everyone who sought his assistance until late into the night, though he would be starting his day in just a few hours. Sometimes this went on untll well past midnight, and he would debate whether he should go to sleep at all, fearful that he would oversleep.

In his later years Rabbi Yosef would speak of the importance of those who departed this world on Hoshana Rabbah. If people only knew how great the value of these people were, they would all desire to depart this world on that day. And so it was. Rabbi Yosef Adas merited that his funeral take place on the eve of Hoshana Rabbah.

RABBI MICHAEL ZERIHAN

Rabbi Michael Zerihan was born in the year 5710 (1950) in Marakesh, Morocco. His father, Rabbi David, was a great *tzaddik*. In 5721 (1961), Rabbi David brought his family to the Land of Israel. The journey was difficult, no less than the difficulties they experienced when they arrived. Eventually Michael found an apartment near Ponoviezh Yeshivah, where he went to study.

As an immigrant, Michael had to learn a new language, and his level of Torah knowledge was lower than that of the Israeli students. But he was blessed with a quick mind and determined to learn, so he exerted himself to bring his learning up to par. In a very short time, he gained the additional knowledge he needed and was able to advance. Soon he became one of the best students in his elementary school. When Grodno Yeshivah in Ashdod opened, Michael was chosen to be one of the first students to be sent from Ponoviezh to establish the new yeshivah. He was very successful there, and he progressed quickly in his learning. After two years Michael returned to Ponoviezh Yeshivah, where his diligence set an example for the other students.

During this time, Michael's father passed away, but even this tragedy could not keep Michael from advancing in his studies. He received a wonderful evaluation from the *gaon* Rabbi Shraga Grossbard, who became Michael's spiritual guide and surrogate father.

The love that developed between Michael and his rebbe was so great that they were together, literally, in both life and death. Years later, two hours after Rabbi Shraga died under emergency care in Tel HaShomer Hospital, Rabbi Michael took ill. Ten days later, he, too, passed away and joined Rabbi Shraga in Heaven.

In addition to his special relationship with Rabbi Shraga, Michael also enjoyed a close relationship with the *rosh yeshivah*, Rabbi Baruch Dov Pobrosky, who liked to discuss Gemara with Michael. Rabbi Baruch was Michael's *shadchan* and, together with Rabbi Shraga, helped find the young couple a place to live. MIchael was about to purchase an apartment in Kiryat Sanz in Netanya, when he was summoned to the home of the Kloisenberger Rebbe so the Rebbe could meet him.

The Rebbe described Michael as a "holy Jew." Indeed, the young man became well known for his righteousness and humility. When they approached Michael to become a rebbe in the yeshivah, he refused, claiming that he was not worthy of such a position because he was not yet sufficiently knowledgeable. He refused even though he was poor, and the salary he would have earned as a rebbe would have eased his financial situation. But his rebbes managed to persuade him to take the position. Rabbi Michael became a devoted teacher, dedicated to educating his students.

Later, Rabbi Michael was appointed to serve as rabbi of the

Gan Berachah and Ramat Herzl neighborhoods. In addition to his responsibilities as a community *rav* and teacher, he opened up several successful afternoon yeshivos for young children in nonreligious neighborhoods. He also participated in outreach programs in Netanya under the auspices of Yeshivas Or Yom Tov.

Rabbi Michael gave lectures to the public, to children as well as adult men and women. When he spoke, his audience was riveted by his beautiful manner of speaking. His words came straight from the heart, and his listeners appreciated his sincerity. Rabbi Michael was devoted to his students and served as both father and advisor to them. He also wrote the five-volume responsa *Ma'ayan Chaim*.

On 24 Cheshvan 5754 (1994), while still in the prime of life, Rabbi Michael passed away, after much pain and suffering.

RABBI SHLOMO ZALMAN AUERBACH

Rabbi Shlomo Zalman Auerbach was born on Shabbos 23 Tamuz 5670 (1910). His father was the *gaon* Rabbi Chaim Yehudah Leib, and his mother was a very righteous woman named Tzivia. They lived in the Sha'arei Chesed neighborhood of Jerusalem.

As a young boy, Shlomo Zalman was recognized as a special child capable of greatness. His parents watched over him carefully to make sure nothing interfered with his Torah studies. His teachers in the elementary school he attended, and later in Eitz Chaim Yeshivah, taught him everything, including *middos*.

While Shlomo Zalman was growing up, the majority of Jerusalem's residents were impoverished. This was especially true of the Auerbach family. But their poverty did not prevent Shlomo Zalman from studying Torah. His friends liked to tell the following story about him:

"When the first car came to Jerusalem, it was called a 'horseless carriage.' Hundreds of people came out onto the streets to get a look at this amazing invention. But there was one person who did not come out — Shlomo Zalman stayed in the *beis midrash*, unwilling to interrupt his studies."

In Eitz Chaim Yeshivah, the students were tested periodically. Shlomo Zalman knew more than anyone else and was tested on entire tractates of the Talmud, which he knew by heart. Those who passed the tests asked for *sefarim* as their prize, but Shlomo Zalman always asked for money. He put the money away, and when he had saved enough, he bought a hearing aid for his mother, who was hard of hearing.

When Shlomo Zalman completed his studies in the elementary school of Eitz Chaim, he went on to the *yeshivah ketanah*. He continued to study Torah with diligence. In fact, the scholars of his neighborhood remarked how, during vacation, Shlomo Zalman could be found in the Gra Synagogue, learning Torah.

When Shlomo Zalman grew older, he became *rosh yeshivah* of Kol Torah yeshivah. After many years as *rosh yeshivah*, Rabbi Shlomo Zalman revealed a glimpse of his life as a youth, how he had studied so diligently.

It happened when one of his students was absent from the yeshivah for several days, and he asked the missing student's study partner where his friend was. "He doesn't feel well," answered the friend. "He has the flu." Rabbi Shlomo Zalman thought to himself, *Just because the boy has the flu he is excused from learning Torah?* Aloud he said to the student, "If I had not studied whenever I did not feel well I would never have learned Torah at all. You cannot imagine how much I suffered in my youth."